ROOMMATES

A STEPBROTHER ROMANCE

Hazel Kelly is the author of several romance novels. She was born in the United States and lives in Ireland.

ALSO BY HAZEL KELLY

The Tempted Series

The Fated Series

The Club Abbott Series

The Wanted Series

The Craved Series

The Devoured Series

The Exposed Series

Available from Amazon.com & Amazon.co.uk.
Also available on Kindle and other devices.

ROOMMATES

A STEPBROTHER ROMANCE

Hazel Kelly

First published 2016.

ISBN-13: 978-1539511762

© 2016 Hazel Kelly

All rights reserved. Except as permitted under the U.S. Copyright Act of 1976, no part of this publication may be reproduced, transmitted, copied, or stored in any form or by any means without prior written permission of the author. Your support of the author's rights is appreciated.

This is a work of fiction. All characters, names, events, brands, companies, and locations in this story are products of the author's imagination. Any resemblance to actual persons, organizations, and settings is purely coincidental.

Printed and bound by CreateSpace.

Cover Artwork – © 2016 L.J. Anderson of Mayhem Cover Creations

"There is always some madness in love.

But there is also always some reason in madness."

- Friedrich Nietzsche

Prologue

I always liked him. I just didn't realize it because I was so awkward back then, especially around guys. I guess I still kind of am.

To make matters worse, I was only fifteen when our parents got married, which made the confusing feelings I had for him- that horrible teenage attraction mixed with extreme repulsion- even worse.

But it wasn't really repulsion at all. The resistance I felt was merely my own lack of confidence coupled with the subconscious understanding that my feelings for him weren't okay.

I'll never forget the anxiety I felt the night a party at Jesse Kandinsky's got so out of control that my theater friends and I actually got in.

Ethan was there. Along with all the other popular kids.

I saw him in the kitchen as soon as I walked in the back door. And he saw me, too. He always saw me. It was talking to me that he avoided.

I stood back from his circle of friends and watched Jesse spin an empty wine bottle on the butcher block while my friend, Brandi, rummaged in her oversized purse for the two bottles of hard lemonade her older sister gave us.

It was obvious that everyone was drunk but me. Yet strangely, even my vision felt blurry as I tried to reconcile the noise and the crowd while clocking my emergency exits.

But when the spinning bottle stopped, the room came into focus again, and I realized everyone was staring at me.

"Looks like you've gotta kiss Jen," Jesse said to Ethan.

I felt the color drain from my face, taking the moisture in my mouth with it as a suffocating panic grew in my chest. I was going to be found out.

Ethan laughed it off. "Yeah, that's not happening. She's my sister."

"Not really, though," Jesse said.

Everyone erupted into nervous laughter and jeering sounds that made the already hostile environment seem even more like a jungle full of predators.

My cheeks felt like they might burst into flames.

"Don't be stupid," Ethan said, tilting a can of beer over his mouth.

When Jesse spun the bottle again, Ethan glanced back at me one more time and wiped the back of his hand across his lips.

I've been wondering what it would be like to kiss him ever since

ONE
- Jenny -

I'd knocked so many times now it was going to be seriously awkward if he opened the door.

I sighed and pulled the spare key from my pocket, letting the yellow lanyard it was on dangle from my palm.

I was afraid this would happen, that he wouldn't be here, that I'd be left standing outside his door with a duffel bag and no invitation.

I nearly jumped out of my skin when my phone rang.

"Hi." I scrunched my face.

"Hey," my stepdad said. "I'm just calling to make sure you arrived okay."

My eyes traced the outline of Ethan's front door. "I'm here, but I don't think he's home."

"He's probably at work. Just let yourself in. That's why I gave you the key." "I know- I just... Does he even know I have it?"

"I'll let him know."

"I don't want him to come home and get spooked when he finds me asleep on the couch."

"Don't be ridiculous. Go inside and relax. So your mom can finally relax."

"Okay."

"And good luck at your audition. We're rooting for you."

"Thanks, Ed."

I slipped the phone back in my pocket and squeezed my eyes shut as I turned the key in the door.

After I pushed it open, I stuck my head in first, relieved that the city lights from outside lit up the room, making it easy for me to find the switch on the wall inside the door. Then I dragged my small bag in from the hall and locked myself inside.

I put my key on the end of the kitchen counter and leaned against it, allowing my body to feel the exhaustion I'd been fighting off all day as I kept to myself on the twelve hour bus from Oberlin.

The apartment was nice despite the fact that it was lacking in any cozy feminine touches- apart from a trace of fresh lemon scent in the air.

There was a black leather couch- my temporary bed presumably- along the back wall of the open room underneath an abstract print of what looked like the silhouette of two women kissing.

I turned my head towards the far end of the kitchen. The top of the fridge was cluttered with a dozen different kinds of liquor bottles and a barrel of whey protein the size of my suitcase.

Before taking my shoes off, I looked down at the floor.

I didn't normally take my shoes off in guy's apartments, but most guys were filthy and shed as carelessly as cats. But the sparkling white tiles on Ethan's kitchen floor looked immaculate.

So either his condo came with a cleaning lady, he had an obsessive compulsive girlfriend, or all those years at boarding school had actually rubbed off on him.

I opened the fridge. It was almost entirely bare. As far as I could tell, he either ate all his meals out or he subsisted on nothing but eggs and BLTs.

I walked over to the closest door. It was locked. I tried it again but had no luck so I let my eyes wander to the black bookcase beside it.

The top two shelves contained books about booze and bartending: Classic Cocktails, 1001 Cocktails to Try Before You Die, The Stout Bible. Below that there were books about street art. I recognized Banksy's name but none of the others.

I squatted down to get a better look at the bottom shelf. It contained a few fiction classics- On the Road, Raisin in the Sun, Catcher in the Rye. And in the corner there was a book called The Third Policeman.

It was the copy I gave him when he went to college. I flipped through it. A few of the pages were folded over. I slid it back on the shelf, wondering why he never mentioned he read it.

Across the room was a cracked door. I walked across the floor and pushed it open. His bedroom was dark and smelled like aftershave. I flicked the light on.

His bed was made with military precision and his closet doors were open, revealing a closet that was ready for a magazine shoot down to the row of shoes along the floor.

I made a mental note to myself to be really tidy so I didn't piss him off, though I imagined it wouldn't make much difference considering he wasn't exactly expecting a house guest.

Atop his dresser, there was a picture of his mom. It was one I'd seen before of her flying a kite in the Outer Banks before he was born.

When our parents got married, my mom had the same one framed and put it up in the family room as a sort of olive branch for Ethan. She wanted him to know that she wasn't going to try and replace his mother, that she understood how much she meant to him.

But despite her best efforts, he never made it easy for her. Still, that was nothing compared to what he put his dad through. I don't think he ever forgave him for remarrying.

Eventually Ethan's anger became difficult to manage. In fact, it got so bad my stepdad actually seemed relieved when he got kicked out of school because it gave him an excuse to send him away.

I was only sixteen then, and I could count on my fingers how many times I'd seen Ethan since.

And while I knew our parents thought sending him away was what was best for him, I never did.

I mean, it's not like he went out of his way to be nice to me, but I never once felt threatened by him or thought he was dangerous.

He was just sad. And I'd be really sad, too, if I went through what he did with his mom. Not that I could relate.

My dad just fucked off when I was a baby. My mom always maintained it was the nicest thing he ever did for me.

I wasn't actively snooping, but I knew I'd crossed the line when I pulled the top dresser drawer open and found a row of folded boxers next to a fishbowl full of condoms.

I closed the drawer and swallowed.

There was only one more door to look behind, and I had to check it because I was bursting to use the toilet.

I wasn't a diva or anything, but I'd never been to New York before, and I didn't want my first experience of the city to be the bathroom at the bus station so I'd forced myself to hold it.

Sure enough, there wasn't a stray pube in sight or a single wet towel on the floor.

Maybe boarding school had been good for him. After all, I'd never seen him fold shit during that year we lived together, never saw him wash a dish, never saw him make his bed- not that I ever stuck my head in his room when he was home.

I hoped he'd be able to see that I'd changed for the better, too.

College had been really eye opening for me. I'd grown up a lot, and I wasn't nearly as naïve or annoying as I once was. He didn't need to be embarrassed by me anymore.

After I went to the bathroom, I pulled a spare blanket out from the top of the closet and double checked that the condom drawer was closed. It was bad enough that I showed up uninvited. I didn't want him to know I'd shown myself around his underwear drawer, too.

Then I turned his bedroom lights off, laid down on the couch, and studied my script until my eyelids got heavy.

TWO
- Ethan -

In my line of work, a guy's got to be careful.

After all, with great power comes great responsibility. And just because I could have my pick of hot drunk girls any night of the week didn't mean taking them up on their advances was always the right thing to do.

Besides, women say a lot of stupid shit when they're drunk, and they're no better than guys. Once they get drunk enough, they'll hit on anything that moves.

So resisting isn't usually much trouble.

But I'm no saint. If a twelve is going to hit on me every night she comes in week after week, eventually I'm going to grow weary of saying no.

Which is how I ended up with my hand wedged between Naomi's thighs in the elevator of my building.

"I thought you'd never take me home," she said, arching her back and lifting her face towards the ceiling, her shiny black braids falling around my face as I bit her slender neck.

"I admire your persistence," I growled, pulling her wet panties to the side.

She was beautiful, like a black Charlie's Angel. And she'd been nursing her drinks all night, wrapping her fat lips around her skinny straw as she watched me work the bar, ignoring her friends and every other guy who made a pass. So there was no doubt she wanted it even more than I did.

Which is exactly how I liked it.

The elevator dinged, and I took a step back. "After you," I said, holding the doors open and sweeping my free hand towards the hall.

She shook her head at me, batting her long eyelashes as her ridiculously short dress flitted inches below her ass.

Hell, with a dress that short, it was only right to make sure she got home safe.

She stuck her hand around and groped me as I fumbled with my keys.

"Hurry up," she said. "Before I change my mind."

I laughed. "As if your mind has anything to do with this." I pulled her in my apartment, closed the door, and slammed her against it, planting my lips on her soft mouth.

She tilted her hips against me and started unbuttoning my shirt.

I slid a hand under the round cheek of her ass and pulled her thigh up against my hip. If I had my way, she'd be showing me exactly how flexible she was in no time.

She moaned in my mouth as I slid my hand back between her legs, picking up where I left off in the elevator.

A moment later I felt her nails against my bare chest, teasing the length of it before she curled them inside the top of my pants.

I pulled my hips back an inch so she could undo my belt, her urgency making my dick swell.

"Ahem."

I froze.

Naomi's eyes were big and still in the dark.

I pressed a finger over my lips so she'd be quiet and lowered her leg as slowly as I could.

She pursed her lips.

I spun around and flicked the light on.

Two sleepy eyes peered over a blanket from across the room.

"Jen?"

She lowered it so I could see her face. "Sorry. If I'd known you were going to have company-"

"What the fuck are you doing here?"

She swallowed as her eyes bounced back and forth between me and… me and… Oh right.

I turned around.

Naomi looked like her eyes were still adjusting to the bright light of my kitchen.

"I'm really sorry," I said. "But it turns out it's not a good time."

She looked so offended I thought I'd been dropped into an episode of Housewives of Atlanta for a second.

"Can I call you a cab or something?" I asked.

Her mouth fell open. "You're fucking serious."

I nodded and reached past her for the handle on the door.

"I thought you were going to show me a good time." Her eyes stabbed me like darts. "What was all that talk about how you were going to lick m-"

"Raincheck," I said, pushing her into the hallway and closing the door.

"Asshole!" she yelled through it.

I kept my hand on the door and dropped my head.

"I'm sorry, Ethan."

I squeezed my eyes shut.

"Your dad was supposed to tell you I was coming."

I couldn't remember the last time I heard her voice, but it hadn't changed, and hearing it made me feel sixteen again.

"It's only for a few days so I can go to this audition and-"

I turned around. "How the hell did you even get in here?"

She raised her eyebrows and pointed towards the counter. "Your dad gave me your spare key-"

"I never gave him-" I snatched the offending key off the counter and banged my fist on it. "God dammit."

She shrank against the couch. "Should he not have-"

"No, he shouldn't have," I said. "He got this made without my permission."

"Maybe he was just trying to be helpful? In case you ever got locked out?"

I glared at her. Was she seriously still so naïve? My dad had never done a fucking thing to help me out in his entire- "What are you doing here again?"

"I have an audition."

"For what?"

"For a role in-"

"Never mind." I raised one hand and pinched my temples with the other. "I can't deal with this shit right now."

When I dropped my hands, she was staring at my chest. Her cheeks turned red.

I sighed. "How long?"

"How long what?"

"How long do you need a place to stay?"

She pursed her lips.

I pulled my belt the rest of the way off, folded it in one hand, and leaned against the counter.

"Just a few days," she said. "If I get a part, I'll look for something more permanent."

I clenched my jaw and inhaled through my nose.

"I'm really sorry again about my timing," she said, nodding towards the door. "I just didn't want things to go any further while I was sitting here and-"

She always was a prude. "Don't worry about it. It's no big deal."

"Still."

I grabbed a glass from the kitchen, filled it with tap water, and drank it down.

She pulled her knees to her chest. "It's good to see you."

"Yeah," I said, walking around the counter towards my bedroom door. "You, too."

But I didn't mean it. Not a fucking word. In fact, every decision I'd made over the last six years was made so I would stop seeing her.

And now here she was in my goddamn apartment. In her pink pajamas. With no makeup on so I could see the freckles on her nose, the same fucking freckles I'd crossed the country to get away from.

"Well, goodnight," she said, her face so innocent she shouldn't have been allowed anywhere near this city.

I nodded and closed the door, wondering what the hell I'd done to deserve this.

All I wanted was to live a simple life filled with simple women who I could entertain simple feelings for.

But apparently I couldn't have that.

Just like I couldn't have Jen.

THREE
- Jenny -

My bladder was full when I woke up.

I rubbed my eyes and rolled over.

Ethan's door was still closed.

Shit. Under no circumstance could I creep in there and use the bathroom if he was in bed. Not after last night.

For all I knew, he slept naked. Or I'd wake him when I flushed. And I couldn't not flush. I mean, I was already an unwanted houseguest.

I scooted to the end of the couch where I'd stashed my bag and pulled my bra out, keeping my eye on his door as I put it on under my pajama top. Then I reached for my phone on the glass coffee table. It was after nine.

I tried to recall when he'd come in the night before, but I hadn't checked. All I knew was that I was dreaming when I heard the door slam. God that was so awkward to see him touching that girl across the room, to hear her moaning like that.

Just thinking about it again sent a chill up my neck.

I folded the blanket I'd used in the night and laid it across the back of the couch, hoping he'd be impressed with my attempt to make my temporary bed. At this stage, I needed to be on my best behavior.

I figured as long as I stayed out of his hair, he wouldn't kick me out. But somehow I knew that wouldn't be enough. I wanted him to like me, not just tolerate me like he always had.

Perhaps a gesture of thanks was in order.

I opened the blinds a little and looked out the window. He had a great view of the city, which was a nice surprise since I half expected his windows to face other walls or grimy dumpsters after the way my stepdad bitched about New York.

He was always saying it was full of shallow social climbers and wannabes and people who thought too highly of themselves. It was his least favorite place on Earth.

Perhaps that's why Ethan had decided to call it home.

Personally, I didn't have an opinion on the place. Not yet. All I knew was that- as an aspiring actress- I could probably be accused of being any one of those things so who knew what he thought about me. But I already knew I was going to love the place, the energy of it, the unpredictability.

Not that I didn't love growing up in Ohio, but I'd always longed for the creative buzz that seemed to spring out of major cities where everything was bigger, brighter, louder, and more glamorous. I just hoped New York would love me back.

Starting today.

Then again, maybe it would be wise to start with winning over my roommate.

I went to the fridge and pulled out the carton of eggs, the bread, the milk, and the butter, tiptoeing as quietly as one of the cat sized rats my stepdad warned me about. I flinched as I pulled a pan from one of the cabinets, as if I could make up for the clanging metal sound by opting not to breathe.

And I'd never been more conscious of the noise a cracking egg makes. Of course, it wasn't until I'd cracked all but two of them that I realized I probably shouldn't have helped myself to Ethan's stuff without asking.

Moments after the first batch of toast popped, the smell hit my nostrils, and I hoped Ethan would wake up soon because I didn't want to have to decide which was less awkward- bringing him breakfast in bed or surprising him whenever he woke up with cold scrambled eggs.

Fortunately, I heard him get up when the eggs were halfway done cooking, and despite my desire to come across as cool and casual, I had to pee so bad at that point all bets were off.

I raised my eyes from the pan when he opened his bedroom door. He was standing shirtless, a pair of navy sweatpants pulling between his hip bones. I felt a shameful curl of heat in my stomach.

Last time I saw him, he still had a few boyish qualities left, a few skinny features here and there. But he'd completely filled out, and he didn't look anything like the thin, metro gay guys I'd studied drama with.

"Morning," he said, speaking through a scratch in his throat.

"Morning," I said, looking back down and wondering if he'd gotten all dressed up for me.

"You're making breakfast."

I raised my eyebrows. "Is that okay? I just thought-"

"I wish you would've asked first."

My heart stopped.

"Those were special eggs."

I looked up at him and turned the burner down. "I'm sorry. I didn't know. I'll-"

"I'm joking, Jesus. The look on your face."

"Fuck you," I said, the heat in my cheeks moving to the back of my neck.

He rolled his eyes. "Relax."

"I was trying to be nice."

"Try to be nice with a thicker skin or you're going to get eaten alive out here."

I hadn't realized how high and hopeful I'd been until he rained on my good vibes. "Can I use your bathroom?"

He pushed his door open and stepped up to the counter. "I don't see why not," he said. "What's mine is yours, right?"

I turned the burner off and walked towards his room.

"My apartment, my couch, my eggs-"

I clenched my jaw as I passed him.

I felt a little less anxious after I went to the bathroom, but I didn't go back to the kitchen right away. Instead, I stared at myself in the mirror and tried to calm myself down.

So what if he didn't like me? Why did I care so much?

My skin was plenty thick enough. I didn't need his approval. I just needed his couch for a few days, and if he wasn't happy about it, so what?

I'd never asked him for a goddamn thing.

Not a ride, not a hug, not even a "hey can you open this for me?"

What right did he have to treat me like this when I hadn't done anything wrong?

Besides maybe cock block him a little last night.

But I said I was sorry.

I took a deep breath and puffed my chest out like a Gorilla until I felt big and proud and strong like my charisma book promised I would- or rather, until I felt silly. Then I headed back out to the kitchen.

And while I wanted to stay mad at him and show him that I could be hard and not cut anybody slack, too, that all went out the window as soon as I saw him again.

Because something about the way the muscles in his arms and stomach moved as he plated those special eggs made me forget everything.

Including the fact that he was totally off limits.

FOUR
- Ethan -

"I've decided to let you stay," I said, forking another clump of scrambled eggs. "Since this breakfast isn't half bad."

She swallowed the bite she was chewing. "I didn't realize you were thinking about kicking me out, but thanks. I'm glad my eggs have helped you decide to do the right thing."

"You're welcome."

"Maybe you could celebrate my good luck by putting some clothes on."

I looked up from my plate.

Her hazel eyes were down on her eggs.

"I thought you were an artiste?"

"I'm an actress."

"A wannabe actress."

"Better than an honest to goodness asshole."

One side of my mouth curled up in a smile.

She raised her eyebrows. "What's your point?"

"No point," I said, leaning back in my chair. "I'm just surprised that a half naked human body would be so offensive to you."

"And I'm surprised you didn't learn some respect after all those years in boarding school."

I narrowed my eyes at her. "Respect? You're the one that showed up here uninvited."

"Your dad said it was okay."

"What the heck does that even mean? You think his lack of consideration for my privacy is an excuse for your rudeness?"

She pulled a knee up to her chest and hugged it. "Look, Ethan. I only need to stay for a few days. I thought it would be okay because I've never asked you for anything."

I blinked at her. I supposed that was true, but she'd demanded so much of my attention over the years it felt like it couldn't be.

"Plus, I would do it for you."

I rolled my eyes.

She raised her eyebrows. "But if I'm really cramping your style so much, just say the word and I'll go."

I bit one of my triangles of toast in half. "Where would you go?"

"I don't know. I'll figure something out if I have to," she said. "But frankly, I'm beyond stressed out over this audition, and I really don't need your shit right now."

I groaned. Why did she have to be so fucking sensitive-to my nakedness, my attitude? Could she not see how severely style cramping that was?

"Well?"

"You don't have to go, okay. I'm not even really mad at you. I'm mad at my dad for having the audacity to copy my fucking key without permission and then lend it out to guests without giving me so much as a heads up."

She pursed her lips.

"You'd think his controlling ways would've lessened considering how long ago I moved out and the fact that I went halfway across the country to get some goddamn space, but he just won't take a hint."

"I know he can be a little intense-"

I furrowed my brow. "A little intense?! He makes Robert De Niro in Meet the Parents look like Mr. Rogers."

"Which is why when he told me to take your key and show up here, I didn't feel like I had a choice."

I stared at her open face. She looked so young in her matching pajamas, so innocent. And I knew she was telling the truth.

After all, I got out.

I'd learned how to say no to my dad after years of practice and distance, distance she never had. And even though he wasn't her father, he was intimidating in a way I can only imagine was hellish for her growing up.

Plus, without me around to distract him, I often worried about how things must've been for her after I left.

But, selfishly, I didn't care. Because even though my dad was a controlling prick, I knew she was safe under his roof, though I admit it never occurred to me that she might ever be under mine.

"You gonna eat that?" I asked, lifting my chin towards her last triangle of toast.

She slid her plate towards me.

"Tell me about your audition," I said.

"Yeah?"

"Sure." I figured I'd given her enough hell for the day, which I had to do because she couldn't stay. She couldn't like it here.

But considering that her time was limited, I might as well get her talking.

After all, maybe if I got to know her, I'd discover that she wasn't all that great anymore and that I'd outgrown my stupid childhood crush on her, a crush I never should've had in the first place.

Cause back then she was a weird drama student teacher's pet who I couldn't be seen to acknowledge, much less like.

And yet, in those days, everything about her was interesting to me: the way she looked in headbands, the way she hummed to herself when she thought no one was paying attention, the stupid pride she took in her grades. She was like another species, and most of the time, I couldn't tell if I was studying her or hunting her.

"One of my professors told me about it. It's the story of the Beach Boys and their rise to-"

"So are you going for the part of Dennis or Brian?"

She cocked her head. "Very funny."

I smiled. I knew androgynous looks were in these days, but Jen couldn't have played a convincing man if she were the best actor in the world.

"To be honest, I'd be happy with anything. I mean, this is my first audition for something this big. If I even get to be an extra I'll be thrilled." She pulled her feet up and sat cross legged. "It would be a relief to have something on my resume besides school productions, ya know?"

I folded my arms across my chest. "So what do you have to do to prove you're the person for the job?"

"I have to read out some lines, sing a bit, and there's a good chance they'll teach me a routine to see how quickly I can pick up choreography."

"Sounds like you'll have plenty of chances to impress them."

"I hope so," she said. "I know it would be lucky to get something so soon after graduation, but I don't really have a Plan B."

"I was never really into Plan B's myself."

Her eyes softened at the edges, and I felt a twinge in my groin.

"So what's Plan A?" I asked. "To become a huge movie star?"

She laughed. "That's sort of Plan A+."

I raised my eyebrows.

"I'd be happy if I could just get enough acting jobs to keep food on the table and not have to go back to Ohio."

"I hear that."

"It's not really fame I'm after. I just want to make a living doing what I love, if that makes sense."

"It does," I said. "And I know exactly what you're talking about."

"Yeah?"

I shrugged. "Of course. I love my job."

She narrowed her eyes at me. "You love bartending?"

"I do."

"Cool."

"You don't have to get it," I said, reaching for her empty plate and stacking it on my own. "Just like I don't have to get what you like so much about showing people your jazz hands."

"I suppose." She stood up and reached for the plates. "Here. Let me."

I watched her wrap her delicate fingers around the stack of dishes. "Thanks," I said, standing up.

She walked around the counter to the sink and turned on the tap.

"You know where you're going today then?"

She started to glance up at me but her eyes only got halfway up my chest before she looked back down at the bottom of the sink. "Yeah. I'm good."

"Great," I said, walking back towards my room. "Well, break a leg."

"Thanks," she said, letting her eyes meet mine for a second.

But as I closed the door to my room, I had a horrible sinking feeling that the only thing at risk of getting broken here was my heart.

All over again.

Just like the day she got cast in the role of my stepsister.

FIVE
- Jenny -

My first impression of New York was that it was a hostile, loud, crazy place that didn't love me back.

I don't know why I'd built it up in my mind as this OZ where the clouds were going to part, the sun was going to shine down on me, and my obvious talent and stage presence would be so apparent as I walked down the street that people would come up and say they were sure they recognized me from somewhere and could they have a selfie and an autograph.

Instead, the overwhelming feeling I had- starting with the first horn that nearly gave me a heart attack- was that I was in everyone's way.

And not only was I in everyone's way, but everyone was far more important than I was and they were headed somewhere far more important than where I was going.

Which made it hard to cling to my energizing hopefulness.

And as misplaced as my positivity probably was, I didn't want to lose it because I knew I didn't stand a chance in this city if I didn't nurture my deluded self-belief.

I'd read enough celebrity biographies to know that the only way I was ever going to make it in show businesses was if I was my biggest fan.

So I couldn't waiver in my confidence. I couldn't doubt my destiny, and I couldn't second guess my right to be here. Otherwise, everyone else would, too.

Like the greats who went before me, I would embrace my triumphs as much as my failures, and I would constantly remind myself that only people who've made it have critics.

After all, if I didn't believe I had talent and that entertaining people was my true calling, I might just curl up under a blanket with a good book and never try to get on stage again.

I certainly wouldn't have climbed the steps onto that bus yesterday, the bus that brought me to the heart of the action and would someday be the bus that starred in my memories as the bus ride that changed it all.

Cause there was no going back.

If I wanted to be somebody someday, I had to keep my chin up despite feeling like this place was going to eat me alive and spit me out.

If only my fearlessness wasn't an act.

If only I were brave like Ethan.

I mean, he was the kind of tough I wanted to be. He didn't give a shit what people thought of him. He did what he wanted to do, and he didn't apologize for it.

I never thought I'd say this about someone that got expelled from school, but I could learn a lot from him.

Sure, I would be fine once the audition was underway. I always was. Being other people was what I was most comfortable with.

It was those few minutes in the beginning when I had to introduce myself and be little ole Jennifer Layne from Middle of Freaking Nowhere, Ohio that terrified me.

And by the seventh time a turning car honked at me, I thought I was going to burst into tears.

Where I was from, nobody ever beeped at anyone- unless it was to get their attention so you could offer them a friendly wave.

But this place was unsympathetic, and while I'd heard people say it was better to be a little fish in a big pond, I was starting to think maybe that saying hadn't been thought through.

I squeezed my way out of the herd of people I was traveling with to catch my breath, feeling like I finally understood what it must be like to be a wildebeest caught in a stampede.

Once I had a bit of much needed personal space, I checked the street signs and then my map. I was only one street away and a full hour early. I put my stuff away, zipped my purse, and backed up against the wall of the department store behind me as I pulled out my phone.

"Hello?"

"Brandi, it's me," I said, covering my open ear so I could block out the chorus of honking taxis.

"Me who?"

"Jen!"

"Oh my god. Jenny Layne. Gosh, I haven't talked to you since you left for New York to become a big star."

"You're hilarious."

"I'm so glad you haven't forgotten the little people in your life now that you're so busy drinking after work with Amy Schumer and Jennifer Lawrence."

I rolled my eyes. "Yes, well. It hasn't been all milk and cookies. Amy can be a bit needy."

"I bet. All the funniest people are."

I cocked my head. "Are you done?"

"Yeah, sure. What's up?"

"My audition is soon, and I need someone to tell me what an awesome big deal I am because it seems like no one in this city got the memo."

"Don't worry," she said. "That's going to make your rapid rise to stardom all the more sweet."

"Go on."

"Just make sure you notice who's the most rude to you so you can snub them once you're a big star."

I laughed. "So far the only person on that list is Ethan, and I'm not sure there's any joy in snubbing someone who wouldn't even notice."

"Is he still the most gorgeous guy on Earth?"

"I don't understand the question."

"Yes you do."

"He's still obnoxious," I said. "Though I guess he did tell me to break a leg, which is, like, the nicest thing he's ever said to me."

"Does he have a girlfriend?"

"I'm not sure girlfriends are really his thing."

"Only because he hasn't seen me in years."

"Yes. I'm sure that's why."

"Do you think if you get the part, he'll let you stay with him?"

"No. I think he's barely prepared to tolerate me for a few days."

"Why is he so awkward around you? You've never done shit to him."

"I know."

"You don't think he knows about that thing you wrote in your diary after-"

"No. I don't. And you're a bitch for mentioning that and for reading my diary in the first place."

"Sorry, but as my best friend, you're required to tell me everything, and I had a feeling you were holding something back."

"But-"

"And you were."

"Yeah, well, I was sixteen, and I had a lot of confusing feelings back then."

"It's okay. It's not like you thought anything I didn't think myself-"

"Moving on swiftly-"

"Oh right. The point is, you're the most beautiful, talented, photogenic person I know, and you're going to absolutely nail your audition."

"Better."

"And not just because it's what you've always wanted, but because then you can move me out to your mansion in L.A., and I can be your personal spray tanner to make sure you always look red carpet ready."

"Of course."

"Instead of having to spend my day tanning all these Midwesterner's cottage cheese thighs."

"I suppose you would really owe me then."

"Quite happily, too."

"Okay, well I better go."

"Me, too. I'm training a new girl today, and if her second victim comes out any worse than the first, we're going to have to change the name of the place to Fifty Shades."

"Yikes."

"Anyway, let me know how the audition goes and give Ethan a big wet kiss for me."

"Absolutely not."

"Fair enough, bitch. Chat soon."

I hung up, put my phone on silent so I wouldn't forget when I got to the audition, and slipped it in my purse.

Then I took off down the street and channeled my inner Gaga all the way to the studio.

SIX
- Ethan -

I saw Christophe's hand shoot up at the back of the restaurant as soon as I walked in.

"Hey," I said, sliding into the wooden booth across from him.

"Dude, are you bleeding?" he asked, pointing at my hand.

I turned my wrist towards me and rubbed the dark red streak. "No, it's just paint." Shit.

"Paint?"

"Yeah. Is Ben coming?"

"What the fuck were you painting?"

"Some asshole dinged my jeep."

He squinted at me. "So you thought you'd paint over it with a different color red?"

"It just dried dark on my hand. Will you let it go? Jesus. Where's Ben?"

"Where do you think?"

I sighed. "Seriously?"

"Yeah."

"He blew us off last week."

He shrugged. "I know."

"I want to be happy for him that he found someone so great, but he's making it really fucking difficult."

Christophe opened the glossy black menu in front of him and sighed. "Women happen to the best of us."

"No shit."

He raised his eyes. "What? Naomi prove a handful last night?"

"Not exactly."

"What's the problem? She told me she wanted to lick your balls till they were raw."

I cocked my head. "Fuck off."

"So she didn't say it," he said. "But she had that look in her eye."

A young girl with a swinging ponytail appeared at the end of the table. "Spicy Nachos?"

"Thanks," Christophe said, scooting his drink over.

She raised her eyebrows. "You guys ready to order?"

"I'll have the bacon burger," Christophe said.

I handed my menu to her. "Same. And a Coke."

She nodded and left.

"So what happened?" he asked. "Last I heard you left together-"

"Things were fine till we got back to mine, but I had an unexpected visitor."

He furrowed his brow and reached for a cheesy chip. "At your place?"

I nodded.

"Who?"

"My stepsister."

"I didn't know you had a sister."

"Stepsister."

"Still."

"Yeah, well, I didn't know you cared."

He raised his eyebrows. "Is she hot?"

I shook my head.

"I'm going to have to take that silence as a yes."

"Take it however you want," I said, sliding a jalapeno covered nacho from the pile between us.

"Can I meet her?"

"She's not your type."

"How so?" he asked. "Cause there's really only two things that would make her not my type."

I furrowed my brows.

He counted on his fingers. "Either she's bald or she doesn't swallow."

I leaned back in the booth and rubbed my painted hand along the edge of the seat. "Yeah, definitely not your type."

"Which is it?"

"Bald," I said. "And gay."

He narrowed his eyes. "Are you fucking with me?"

"Would I joke about having a bald, gay houseguest?" I asked. "Don't you think if I had a gorgeous girl staying at mine I'd be rubbing it in your smug face?"

"Mmm. Probably."

"Plus, you know I like girls with flavor," I said. "Like Naomi."

"True."

But it wasn't. I liked Jen. But going for girls that reminded me of her just made things worse. So I did everything I could to keep my distance from petite brunettes with hazel eyes and melodic laughs. Because it was hard enough to not think about her as it was.

"So," he said. "How long's she staying with you?"

The young waitress placed my Coke on the table a second later.

I turned to offer her some thanks, but she'd already disappeared.

"Well?" he asked.

I shrugged. "I don't know. She's got some audition to go to. She's just staying with me while she sees that through."

"You guys close?"

"Not really. I was sixteen when our parents got married, and I got shipped off to boarding school a year later-"

"So you didn't know her before your folks hooked up?"

"I knew of her."

He raised his eyebrows and drank from his glass, ignoring the straw in it so it poked him in the cheek.

"We went to the same high school," I said. "So I'd seen her around for a while."

"Too bad you guys didn't hit it off."

"Why?"

"Cause then you could've dated all her friends and-"

"We didn't really run in the same crowds."

"So she was a loser?"

"She wasn't a loser," I said too defensively. "She just didn't care about fitting in."

"Because she couldn't if she wanted to?"

"Because she liked books and acting and didn't have an athletic bone in her body."

"When was the last time you talked to her?"

"This morning."

"Before that."

I rolled my eyes up to the ceiling. "When I went home for Christmas her freshman year of college."

"Sounds pretty fucking awkward."

"It's not so bad," I said. "She's cool. A total cock block, but cool."

"Maybe you could find a girl you were both into and-"

I raised a hand. "I'm going to stop you there before you say something that makes me want to punch you in the face."

"Why? It's not like you're related."

I leaned an elbow on the table. "You know who else I'm not related to?"

"Who?"

"Your sister," I said, craning my neck forward. "How's she doing?"

"That's none of your fucking business."

"I thought she kind of took a shine to me last time she came to the club."

"I'm sure she didn't."

"In fact, I think she would've done a lot more than take a shine if I'd-"

He raised his hands in the air between us. "Okay. I get your point. I won't say shit about your sister anymore."

"Stepsister."

"Whatever. Just don't even think about Camille," he said. "Okay?"

"Deal."

"She's too good to be fodder for your pathetic wank bank."

"I assure you that she's-"

He pointed at me. "I'll fucking kill you if you finish that sentence."

I wanted to smirk, but I knew it would set him off so I let it go. Of course, I had zero confidence he wouldn't mention Jen again at some point, but if he could refrain for the rest of the meal, it would be a small grace for which I would be grateful.

"You know what she's auditioning for?"

I raised my eyebrows. "I thought we were done."

"Hey," he said, showing me his palms. "I'm only asking because my uncle's got an agency in Midtown."

I swallowed the nacho in my mouth. "Really?"

"Yeah," he said. "So if she needs some representation-"

"Thanks. I'll keep that in mind."

"I can't guarantee anything, but I can get her an appointment."

"Let's wait and see how the audition goes today," I said. "I'm not sure I want to give her loads of reasons to stick around."

SEVEN
- Jenny -

I thought I'd be able to go home right after the audition, but when the director said the callback results would be up in two hours, I decided to stay in the neighborhood.

The waiting was nerve wracking, though.

Despite my best efforts, I didn't have a clue how I'd fared in the audition, and I could tell by some of the looks I got from the other girls that I wasn't going to be winning any popularity contests.

Brandi always maintained that I had resting bitch face if I wasn't careful, but I wasn't a bitch. I was just shy, especially when I was surrounded by people whose baby toes had more confidence than me. I mean, one girl was name dropping so hard I felt like I should recognize her.

Fortunately, I had my kindle and a healthy appetite to distract me from the stress of waiting to hear whether they wanted to see me again.

God I hoped they did.

It would be so embarrassing to have to tell my mom and my professor and Brandi that I'd flubbed everything up. I knew she was only joking that I was her ticket out of our one tanning salon town, but it was sort of true, and if I did make it big, I wanted to be one of those stars that had all their same childhood friends… so I'd have someone to hang out with when I wasn't playing drinking games with Amy Schumer.

And of course it would be nice to have good news for Ethan so he didn't feel like he'd put me up for nothing. Plus, getting a callback might make him take me more seriously.

I knew he thought I was still the same nerdy girl who co-directed Bye Bye Birdie in high school and read books about the golden age of Hollywood, but I wasn't completely talentless. I mean, I had to cry in a production I did last year.

Surely that counted for something.

I managed to find a little cafe within a few blocks of the studio, and since I didn't have to do any more dancing or singing for the day, I ordered myself a New York sized chocolate milkshake and a chicken sandwich to enjoy while I read.

The milkshake was so delicious I was almost sexually aroused by it, and the sandwich was the perfect thing to nibble mouse sized chunks of in order to keep the table.

After all, I was in no hurry to start wandering the city streets without somewhere to go when I was liable to get trampled.

And as ridiculous as it was, I felt like I'd already made it.

I mean, I was on a veritable lunch break in downtown New York City a few blocks away from a studio where I'd just auditioned for a role in a real Off Broadway production. It was an amazing high.

Sure, I felt like a big girl when I went away to school, but this was different. I'd finally done something that most people never do, and that made me feel special. Like the whole trip had been worth it. Like no matter what happened now, I was one step closer to sticking my hands in cement on Hollywood Boulevard.

And the people watching was amazing.

I'd never seen so many severe bobs and wacky glasses and amazing coats. Everything was bolder and louder and more colorful, and I so desperately wanted to fit in. And yet, it seemed the only way to fit in was to stand out.

No wonder Ethan left and never came back.

I felt like I finally understood.

This place was the total opposite of living in Ohio under his dad's inflexible military standards or the regimented atmosphere of boarding school. It was wild and alive and exciting and unpredictable.

Better.

And I couldn't help but feel like I was in a position to appreciate it more than anyone who'd ever taken such vibrancy for granted.

When enough time had passed that I didn't think I'd be the first person to come looking for the callback list, I paid for my lunch, slipped out the door, and walked purposefully back to the studio, finding that if I just focused on squaring my shoulders directly behind the person in front of me, I was less liable to get knocked around.

And as I approached the typed list in the middle of the large corkboard, my heart was beating in my throat.

I held my breath as my eyes scanned the names of the people who'd earned a second audition, reading slowly to make sure I wouldn't miss a single letter.

And then there it was- my name. Next to a time to return. Next to the part I'd be competing for.

But it didn't say chorus line.

It didn't say surfer girl #4.

It said Marilyn.

I blinked.

Then I blinked some more.

Then I stepped up to the list and dragged my finger under my name and the time and the role just to be sure I was reading straight across the line.

I looked around. People in leg warmers and black turtlenecks and Victorian costumes scurried around the entry way. Going places.

Like me.

But I still had my doubts.

What if it was a mistake?

What if I told my family I was up for a leading role and it was just a typo?

I hoisted my backpack over one shoulder and walked up to the front desk where a woman with jet black hair sat with lime green glasses perched on the end of her nose.

"May I help you?" she asked without looking up.

"Hi, yeah. I have a question about the auditions for Life's a Beach."

"They were this morning."

"I know. I was there."

She lifted her eyes and pointed a pen towards the corkboard. "The callback list is over there."

"I know. I'm on it."

She kept her eyes on a computer screen I couldn't see. "Congratulations."

"I just want to make sure there hasn't been a mistake."

"If there were any mistakes, their names aren't on the list. That's how this works."

"But I'm on there for Marilyn, and it's a leading role."

She straightened up and looked down her nose at me. "Let me guess. This is your first audition in the big city?"

I nodded.

"Thought so. Listen-"

"Jennifer. Jennifer Layne."

"As I was saying, I hope I have a reason to remember your name someday, but unfortunately I already forgot it."

I forced a smile.

"And as far as the list, the person who made it isn't a lowly illiterate volunteer. They're a professional, a professional whose job it is to make sure that list is error free. In fact, his job depends on it. So how about you trust him to do his job, and we'll trust you to do yours which is to come back here- when?"

"Two thirty on Thursday."

"Fabulous. So you can read, too. Just like the man who made the list."

"Okay, thanks for your help," I said, taking a step back from the desk.

Because a cartwheel would've seemed too eager.

EIGHT
- Ethan -

Just her presence in the city was driving me crazy.

When she was back in Ohio, it was easy to tell myself there were no feelings there, that even if there were, she was happy sipping overpriced cappuccinos with a bunch of men in black turtlenecks, offering encouragement in their latest attempts at method acting.

But she hadn't become the weirdo I'd hoped.

On the contrary, she was even sweeter and more beautiful than she was the day I met her.

It was the first week of my sophomore year of high school. I remember getting on the bus and making eye contact with her. And she scooted over.

I don't know if she wanted me to sit with her or if she was just being polite, but she obviously didn't know that I had a seat at the back that my friends made it their business to protect.

I never said anything to her about it, never acknowledged the gesture. Instead, I just made my way to my seat and spent the rest of the week wondering what it would've been like if I'd sat next to the girl with the freckles and the partially eaten candy necklace.

In my mind, she smelled like candy, but I never got close enough to know for sure.

I had other chances, too, moments when I could've gotten to know her. But I chickened out every time. She was too strange, too disinterested in fitting in.

And that was suspect, especially in the small minded place we grew up.

Forging any kind of bond with her could've been social suicide.

For both of us, as many of my so called friends back then could be terribly cruel. And I knew it. But as a teenager, you don't get to pick your friends. You might get to pick one or two if you're lucky, but everyone else comes with the territory and you make do.

So I kept my distance, convincing myself that it was the best thing I could do to protect her- like a scientist who discovers a rare bird in the rainforest and decides not to tell anyone so no harm will come to it.

And then our parents got married and protecting her became my job officially. It was a job she never realized was mine, though it was one I took very seriously.

But she still had that aloof naivety about her. Somehow she hadn't lost it, which was crazy.

I thought college could've beat that willingness to trust people out of anyone. But not her.

Because she was different.

And here I was again kicking myself for not realizing it when I might've actually been able to do something about it.

Like kiss her. Just once.

Cause I'd had years to think about the situation, and as far as I could tell, there were two options.

Either I only thought I wanted her because I couldn't have her, or I was genuinely attracted to her soft features and her quirky personality.

Over the years, I'd picked up tons of women who were easy on the eyes, and I could always tell as soon as I kissed them if there was anything there, if they were worth the trouble. And frankly, if I thought I could get Jenny out of my system with a simple kiss, I probably would've made a move a long time ago.

In fact, it probably would've been the best fucking thing to ever happen to me because then I wouldn't have had to deal with the heavy, unrequited chemistry that stuck like a thorn in my side from the moment my dad told me he was going to marry her mom.

Sure, my confusing crush on her was only part of why I was horrified at his news. If anything, the disgust I had for my dad was the overwhelming emotion that came over me at the time, clogging my throat like black tar.

I remember it like it was yesterday. He told me in the car.

We used to do this thing on Sunday mornings where we'd go for pancakes and then drop flowers off at my mom's grave.

I hated everything about it… and not just because it was one more thing my dad made me do that I didn't want to do.

I didn't even like pancakes. What's more, knowing I was about to go visit my mom's grave didn't exactly do wonders for my appetite.

Of course, he and I never had much in common. In fact, he was genuinely ashamed of some of the things I liked to do- namely drawing- whereas my mom always encouraged me and made a big fuss about the pictures I made for her growing up.

After she died, he took all my pictures down and would flip out if he caught me sketching. He'd say "Who are you fucking drawing those pictures for?! Your mom's dead. What are you stupid?"

It was pretty shit. And yeah, I understood that he was hurting, but I was hurting, too.

Anyway, we were on the way home from one of our Sunday visits to her grave. We gave her daisies that day. My dad let me pick them out. I was so happy that I remembered what she thought about them, especially since I was terrified of forgetting things about her.

I still am.

I was helping her hang sheets to dry in the backyard. We had a dryer, but when the weather was nice, she liked the sheets to smell of fresh air. That was the day she told me she liked daisies because admiring them was the closest she could get to staring at the sun.

I didn't understand why a person would want to stare at the sun, but like any kid, my mind ran away with the idea.

After that, I used to bring her yellow daisies whenever I could find them. Not only because I knew she liked them, but because I was worried that if she didn't have some, she might be tempted to look at the sun instead.

Then she might go blind, and if that happened, she wouldn't be able to see my drawings anymore.

The point is, we were driving back from the graveyard when my dad told me he was going to marry Jen's mom.

I lost it.

After all, it had only been a year since my mom's accident. How my dad could even suggest that he had feelings for another woman was beyond my comprehension... along with how he could've possibly gotten another woman to fall for him. The fact that he ever wooed my mom seemed miraculous enough.

I told him right then and there that if he got remarried, I would never forgive him.

And I did a good job keeping my promise for a long time.

But as I got older, I started to understand that my dad was one of those men who was better off with a woman.

It softened him.

Not much, but enough to make a difference.

And as hard a pill as it was for me to swallow that he was ready to move on with his life, it beat those sad fucking pancakes.

NINE
- Jenny -

Initially, I was over the moon. In fact, I can't be sure, but I might've skipped all the way home. That is, if my feet even touched the ground.

I couldn't recall any hostility on my way back to Ethan's, couldn't recall getting honked at.

Sure, one guy flipped me the bird, but I flipped it right back with a big smile on my face so he'd know that his attempt to drag me down had been fruitless.

After all, the part of Marilyn was one of the only speaking female roles in the show. It was a big enough role that the program would have my headshot in it next to a little bio about me that described the show as my "debut."

To say the prospect of that excited me was a huge understatement.

Of course, that all changed when I started rereading Marilyn's lines. Not that the lines put me off. Rather, it was the stage direction, namely the stage direction in Act One, Scene 7 when she's supposed to kiss Brian Wilson for the first time.

My heart sank in my chest as I pulled my feet up onto the couch.

What if I had to do the kissing scene in the audition itself?

I mean, it was one thing to get lines right when they were my responsibility, but a kiss was a totally different animal. It involved another person, and not only could another person's awkwardness ruin my audition, but what if they had a cold sore or something?

Could I point it out?

That probably wouldn't be professional, but I didn't really want to be the kind of person that had to suck on cold sores to get work.

I guess it was a matter of how far I was willing to go to get the role.

Logically, I knew I'd probably have to kiss someone in my career eventually. I just didn't think it would be so soon.

And when the time came, I'd hoped it would at least be someone gorgeous… like one of the Hemsworth brothers or someone hilarious like Paul Rudd, preferably in a tragic romantic comedy that would really showcase my range.

Unfortunately, I wasn't sure my range extended to acting like I wanted to kiss someone I wasn't attracted to.

I guess I'd just have to picture someone I was attracted to and hope my costar had the decency to keep some mints on hand.

I sighed and reread the stage directions.

It was supposed to be a passionate kiss, a kiss so convincing the audience wouldn't be surprised to discover the characters were married in the very next scene.

Shit.

I closed my eyes and rubbed my temples, trying to recall if I'd enjoyed any kisses that might inform my performance.

There was Jimmy Watts on Prom Night.

Of course, he ended up moving to Vegas to be a showgirl- or so I heard enough times that it must be true. And that was a shame really because he was one of the only guys at my high school who I didn't find repulsive… and who actually knew my name.

Then there was Tim Tomlinson freshman year of college, but he was so busy groping my boobs like an animal I hardly remember if his mouth had done anything interesting.

If there was anyone I might've practiced with more, it might've been him, but when I wouldn't sleep with him the third time we hung out, he told me I was "a self-impressed prude that wasn't good enough to suck his cock, much less sit on it."

I liked to think I dodged a bullet there.

Then there was my T.A. in Foreign Relations who told me that- while he really enjoyed my company and would be happy to take our relationship to a physical level if it was important to me- he identified as asexual.

Needless to say, that didn't exactly make me want to get naked and jump his bones.

After that, I wouldn't say I lost hope or anything. I just sort of threw myself into areas where I'd had significantly more success- like acting, fundraising, and my studies.

And to be honest, I never really had any fear of missing out because I knew exactly what I was missing out on from having roommates, and I was fine with it.

In fact, never once did I have a roommate describe a one night stand without disdain, regret, disappointment, or distinctly boozy morning after breath.

And it was just as well that sexual adventures weren't something I was in a hurry to have because most of my male friends were gay, and nothing destroyed the prospect of sex with straight men like being surrounded by gay ones.

In my experience anyway.

So perhaps the truth of it was that I was less worried about kissing a stranger in the audition than I was about being found out for my total lack of experience.

But how hard could it be?

Assuming the guy playing Brian and I both had normal lips, decent breath, and didn't try anything unconventional with our tongues- like Jimmy the Showgirl did- then it would probably be fine.

Still, the prospect of losing a part for being a bad kisser was a potential career obstacle that had never occurred to me before.

Worst of all, there was no one I could talk to about it.

Brandi would only make a joke out of it. I could practically hear her telling me to go get my tongue pierced and not be afraid to use my teeth.

My mom had no idea how inexperienced I was. In fact, she was so concerned that my stepdad's strictness stifled my willingness to be open with her that she'd hidden packs of birth control pills in my room at college every time she visited.

And my friends at school all thought I had a long distance boyfriend because that's what I told them so they would leave me alone.

So it looked like I'd finally stumbled upon my acting kryptonite.

Crying I could do. I had loads of experience with that. However, swapping crying for kissing would probably do the opposite of impress the director.

Screaming, dancing, singing, laughing, and seizuring were some of the other things I was confident doing on cue.

But kissing, well, I'd be lying if I said I wasn't a little panicked.

After all, having my picture in that program next to my bio was as close as I was going to get anytime soon to seeing my name in lights.

So I either had to spend the rest of the day watching kissing montages, which seemed unnecessary considering how many times I'd seen The Notebook.

Or I had to practice, and I was a little too old to make out with my own hand.

I rolled onto my side on the couch, figuring the best I could do was get really attached to the idea of kissing someone specific so that when the time came, at least my acting- if not my kissing- would be convincing.

A moment later, I heard the key in the door.

And when I looked up, the first person I ever wanted to kiss walked through it.

TEN
- Ethan -

I saw her curled up in one corner of the couch as soon as I walked in.

She was the only feminine thing about the place and stuck out like a sore thumb.

I pulled my headphones out and let them dangle over my shoulder. "Hey."

"Hi," she said. "I didn't know you were a runner."

I unclipped the iPod from my sleeve, turned it off, and set it on the counter with my headphones. "I wouldn't say I'm a runner."

She furrowed her brow. "But you run?"

"Yeah." I walked to the fridge, pulled a bottle of water out, and slammed as much as I could.

"What's the difference?"

I shrugged. "I'm not addicted to it."

She set a stapled stack of papers on the coffee table in front of her. "I didn't realize runners were addicts."

"They are," I said. "Whereas I don't do it all that often, and I could quit tomorrow." Assuming I never got stressed the fuck out again by surprise houseguests who made me feel like I had to take extreme precautions just to manage my own goddamn hormones.

"I see."

I lifted my shirt up and wiped the sweat off my brow. When I dropped it again, she was scrunching her face at me.

"Does my sweat offend you?"

"No," she said. "It just makes me feel kind of bad about the gallon of milkshake I drank this afternoon."

I took my shirt off and used it like a washcloth to wipe my chest and the back of my neck. Then I slung it over one shoulder.

"So," she said, pulling the fallen strap of her black tank top up. "What did you do today?"

I topped my water bottle up at the sink. "Bits and pieces, lunch with a friend, worked out."

She leaned up and crossed her legs. "Is that pretty typical for you?"

"Yeah. Then I work at night."

"Not a bad routine," she said. "Doing what you want all day."

"Beats the alternative," I said, drinking some more water and catching a lose drop with the back of my hand. "How did your audition go?"

She pursed her lips. "Sort of bittersweet."

I raised my eyebrows and walked around to sit on one of the barstools on the other side of the counter, trying to keep my distance out of respect for her comparative cleanliness. "Why? What happened?"

"I got a callback."

"Isn't that a good thing? Doesn't that mean they want to see you again?"

She nodded. "Yeah, and for a decent part, too. I'd have lines and everything if I got it."

"So what's the bad news? Who you have to blow to get the part?"

"Very funny," she said. "But you're not totally off base."

I craned my neck forward. "What?"

She raised a hand when she saw my face drop. "Whoa. I didn't mean- I don't really have to blow anybody. Obviously."

I felt my shoulders relax again.

"I might have to kiss somebody, though."

Why didn't I feel any better? "Who?"

She raised her palms to the ceiling. "Don't know. Suppose I won't know until he's standing there in front of me."

I scrunched my face.

"At which point I'll have to focus on the role I'm trying to play instead of whether he has herpes."

I felt a chill run up my neck.

"Yeah. That's sort of how I feel."

"I suppose this kind of thing was going to happen eventually if you want to go into this line of work."

"I know," she said, casting her eyes down. "I was just hoping I'd have a lot more experience by then."

A hundred questions flashed through my mind like sparks. "What do you mean?"

I shrugged. "I've never had to kiss someone I wasn't attracted to before."

"Right."

"You have any tips for me?"

"Let me see," I said, extending my hand towards the script on the table.

She stood up and smoothed her jean skirt down.

I looked away when she bent over to grab the script because I didn't trust myself not to look down her shirt.

"Here," she said, bringing it to me. "The scene I'm talking about starts at the bottom of this page and goes on to the next one."

I took it and skimmed the text while she slid onto the barstool beside me. "I take it you're Marilyn?"

"Maybe," she said. "If I don't blow it on Thursday."

I turned the page and kept reading. Sure enough, Brian and Marilyn kiss halfway down the page.

"I assume it has to be more than a peck because they're married in the very next scene."

"Yeah," I said, reading the part with the kiss again and doing everything I could not to hope she wouldn't get it. What the fuck was wrong with me?

"So," she said. "Any advice?"

"Act your ass off?"

She rolled her eyes.

"Seriously." I set the script on the counter and leaned back. "There's a good chance whatever thespian you have to kiss to get this part is going to have total dick breath."

"Dick breath?"

"Yeah. From eating-"

"I got it," she said, raising her hand. "Thanks for your help anyway."

I sighed. "You're right. That probably wasn't the support you were looking for."

She cocked her head. "Ya think?"

"So practice with me once."

Her eyes grew wide. "Practice what with you?"

"The scene. The kiss. Whatever."

She swallowed.

"I'm perfect." I slid off my chair and held my arms out. "Especially right now when I'm at my grossest."

She looked me up and down, her face suddenly pale.

"If you can pretend to be attracted to me right now, there's no question you can be convincing with anyone else. After all, who are you less attracted to than me?"

A nervous smile cracked her face. "I suppose you have a point."

"I thought so." I tossed my sweaty shirt on the counter. "Plus, I don't have herpes."

"Are you sure?"

I furrowed my brow. "Of course I'm fucking sure-"

"No I mean-" She shook her head. "What about-"

I squinted at her. "What about what?"

"Our parents?"

I ran a hand through my hair. "Jesus, Jenny. Who gives a shit? I wasn't going to call them up and tell them."

"Right."

"Do you want my help or not?" I asked, my eyes bouncing from her to the clock. "Cause I have to shower and eat and get to work in the next-"

"Okay," she said, sliding off her stool and laying her hand on the script. "But only if you're really going to take it seriously because I can do crappy practice on my own."

"I'll do my best."

"Okay," she said, handing the script to me. "You be Brian."

I raised my eyebrows. "I thought you'd pick up more pointers if I was Marilyn."

She groaned.

"I'm kidding, okay. That was a joke."

She shook her head.

"What?"

"Nothing," she said, her arms hanging at her sides. "It's just that this is important to me, and your jokes aren't helping."

"Okay. Sorry. Just give me two seconds to get into character." I turned around, squeezed my eyes shut, and tried to ignore the alarm bells going off in my head.

"Whenever you're ready," she said.

I looked over my shoulder. "You know your lines?"

She nodded. "Of course. I've been practicing them all day."

ELEVEN
- Jenny -

All I could think about was spin the bottle at Jesse Kandinsky's house.

Did Ethan remember that?

Did he remember completely ignoring me in front of everybody when the prospect of kissing me came up?

I suppose it was better than if he'd laughed in my face.

Of course, I couldn't shake the feeling that that was exactly what was about to go down here. In his kitchen. Seven years later.

At the same time, his willingness to do a read through with me was a welcome surprise. If anything, it confirmed the idea that a little fake kiss was nothing to be worried about.

And if he wasn't freaked out about it, I wasn't going to make a scene. After all, we were both adults. We weren't related. And he was pretty gross right now.

Except I didn't mind the smell of his sweat, the way it made the hairs on the back of my neck stand up. And I certainly wasn't disgusted by his chiseled abs or the way his shorts hung off his protruding hip bones.

To be honest, I was more attracted to him than anyone else on the planet, but I couldn't say that. If I refused to kiss him he'd either think I was a prude, or worse, that I wasn't repulsed by him.

And surely that would cause a lot more problems for me than just letting him think he was helping me out.

"You don't have to memorize your lines," I said. "It's fine if you just read them. I'm the one that has to be convincing."

He nodded but didn't turn around.

I wiped my clammy hands on my skirt and watched the muscles shift in his back as he turned the page.

"Okay," he said, turning around. "I'm ready."

My heart was racing.

"Do you want me to talk like a surfer dude or-"

I narrowed my eyes on his. "Your regular voice is fine."

"Suit yourself," he said, squaring up to me.

I took a deep breath.

He stared at me.

I glanced at his lips.

He raised his eyebrows.

I nodded at the script in his hand.

"Oh right- me first..." He dragged his large finger across the paper and mumbled to himself. "Okay. I got it."

I sighed.

He read his line and I started reciting the ones I'd memorized.

His turn.

My turn.

His turn.

My turn.

His turn.

My turn.

His turn.

"I knew from the moment I heard your music that I wanted to meet you," I said.

"Meet me?" Ethan asked, glancing between me and the script. "Is that all you wanted to do?"

I clasped my hands in front of me. "Actually, I knew when I saw you perform that I'd never be happy just meeting you."

Ethan stepped up to me and looked me in the eyes. "What would make you happy, Marilyn?"

I cast my eyes down at his chest and tried to imagine a Hawaiian shirt in its place. "I'm afraid it wouldn't be very ladylike of me to say."

"Then I'll have to read your lips," he said, dropping the script and putting his hands on my shoulders.

My eyes bounced back and forth between his. "Well, that's music to my ear-"

And then he laid one on me.

I went limp as soon as his lips touched mine. At first, he just held them there, but a moment later, he opened his mouth and slipped his tongue in mine.

He tasted like sweat and it made me thirsty, but I couldn't pull away as he swirled his tongue deeper and grabbed my face.

I put my hands on his bare chest to brace myself as a curl of warmth rose through my center like a trail of smoke.

Then he pulled away, and my breath hitched as I opened my eyes.

He was staring at me with a funny look on his face, an uncertain look I'd never seen before.

I pursed my lips.

"See," he said. "No big deal."

I let my eyes fall down to his lips for a moment before raising them back up to his dark eyes.

"You got this," he said. Then he grabbed his sweaty shirt off the counter, walked in his room, and closed the door.

I looked over my shoulder towards his bedroom and raised my fingers to my lips, knowing that if I could recreate that kiss, the part would be mine.

But there was no way.

Because I hadn't done any kissing there whatsoever.

I had been kissed.

And I had been kissed so good my mind went blank.

Was my acting just so good that the kiss seemed real?

Or had I actually just gotten butterflies from kissing my stepbrother?

I leaned over, picked up the script, and turned to the part about the kiss. Sure, the stage direction said "Brian gives Marilyn a passionate kiss," which explained why Ethan sank his fingers into my soft arms and why he held my face.

But I'm not sure it explained the tongue.

Was tongue really called for?

I suppose it was probably implied by the word "passionate."

But while part of me thought Ethan had missed his true calling for how convincing his performance was, another part of me was skeptical.

Because that kiss wasn't merely French. It was intense.

And as much as his tongue had swirled around mine, I still felt like he was holding back, like I could feel an energy coming off his body that heated me from the inside out.

I put the script on the counter and grabbed a glass from the cupboard.

A moment later, I heard the shower go on.

I filled my glass from the sink and tried not to think about Ethan stripping down on the other side of the wall, tried not to think about him washing himself moments after we'd just shared the most delicious, interesting, addictive kiss of my life.

A kiss I would never mention again to anyone, least of all him.

Cause it shouldn't have happened.

I knew that now.

Granted, if I'd felt nothing at all afterwards, I wouldn't have thought twice about it.

But I didn't feel nothing.

I felt everything.

And all the good things I felt were butting heads with the shame and the guilt and the knowledge that how I felt about what just happened was even less okay than the fact that it did.

I mean, was what we'd done even legal?

He'd fled the scene so quickly I can only assume he thought it was wrong, too.

Or at least that it felt wrong.

Because it felt so right.

And it wasn't supposed to feel like anything.

I took a deep breath, gripped the edge of the counter, and wondered what kind of freak I was that I'd enjoyed his physical attention so much.

Then I tilted the glass of water against my mouth and swallowed my stepbrother's kiss.

TWELVE
- Ethan -

No big deal my ass.

I knew when a kiss wasn't a big deal.

Kissing Naomi, for example, had been a lot like paint by numbers.

I put my hands on her hips and my lips on her mouth and had every intention of kissing her for a polite amount of time before she felt I'd shown her enough respect that she would consider kissing me somewhere else.

But there was nothing polite on my mind when my lips met Jen's.

So much for the levelheaded calm I felt after my run.

That all went out the window as soon as she was close enough for me to smell her candy scent.

What the hell was I thinking?

I tilted my face under the showerhead and let the cold spray sober me up.

I didn't normally take cold showers, but if the water had been even slightly warm, my hard on would've gotten the best of me, and rubbing one out to the thought of her kiss when she was on the other side of the wall was a line I wasn't ready to cross.

Kind of like kissing her, but I'd blown through that red light without so much as a second glance, confirming my greatest fear.

Not only did I want her because I couldn't have her, I wanted her because she was as delicious as she was beautiful.

And she didn't even know it.

Shit. I don't even think she really expected me to kiss her.

But I had to.

Not going through with it would've made the whole thing a big deal. A big, awkward deal.

And I didn't want that.

Seeing as she was effectively going to be my roommate for at least a few more days, the last thing I wanted was to feel awkward in my own goddamn apartment.

Fuck.

I sighed and turned the nozzle just enough to take the iciness out. Then I poured some body wash in my palm and tried to guess what she was thinking.

Probably nothing.

Or she was questioning why I fled the room so abruptly after our read through. Not that she'd ever ask, which was good. Cause telling her I'd come down with the first unruly boner I'd had since I was fourteen probably wouldn't make things less awkward.

I rinsed myself off and stepped out of the shower, doing my best to ignore the nagging ache in my balls as I wrapped a clean towel around my waist.

I wondered if I was better or worse than she thought I'd be.

After all, I knew kissing me must've crossed her mind at some point because a year after I left for boarding school, I came home for Christmas and saw the proof with my own eyes.

I never should've snooped, but I did a lot of questionable shit back then. I didn't think I was a bad person. I just considered the subject of my morality a flexible one.

And when I got home that day, everyone was out. So I did that thing people always do when they know they're home alone. I called everyone's name while I pushed open all the doors in the house just to be sure.

Of course, if Jen had been there, I never would've touched her bedroom door.

But as soon as I did, I saw a notebook sticking out from under her pillow. It looked as if she'd left in a hurry but wasn't worried about anyone coming in her room, which meant they'd likely gone somewhere together as a family.

I remember hoping it was the grocery store because I was so fucking sick of cafeteria food I could've forked my own eyes out.

Anyway, without even giving myself a chance to consider doing the right thing, I crossed the room and slid the journal out from under her pillow.

As I flipped through it- because that seemed a lesser offense than starting from the beginning- my eyes mostly caught words that were uninteresting- homework, drama, queen, psycho, sad, hurts, funny.

But then I saw my name. Actually, it wasn't my name. It just said E.

So naturally, I had to keep reading to see if I was E. And I hoped I was. Because it said "last night I touched myself for the first time like Brandi told me to. But it only felt good when I started thinking about E. Does that make me a bad person? I came and everything. Can I go to hell for that?"

I think my first thought was something derogatory about Brandi, and my second thought was the realization that she fucking wanted me back.

But that's not the most shameful part of the story.

The worst bit is that I slid the journal back under her pillow where it was, stole a pair of her underwear from her underwear drawer, and stroked my dick with them until I came.

Needless to say, I don't think I looked her in the eye a single time over Christmas break.

And it killed me that I couldn't take her aside and tell her that she wasn't going to hell, that an angel like her would never get in.

But that was a long time ago. Shit, I don't even know if "E" was me. But why else would she think it was wrong? Unless some idiot told her masturbation was sinful?

I'd never know.

The point was, I had jerked it to the thought of her more times than I was proud of, and knowing there was a chance she'd thought of me like that kept me in wet dreams for years.

But maybe it wasn't so much wrong as it was inconvenient.

Still, it was too late for anything more to happen.

Our parents had been married for years at this point, and she'd lived under my tyrannical father's roof for longer than I could imagine. Frankly, I'm surprised she'd ever kissed anyone with him as man of the house.

Regardless, it didn't matter how much I still wanted her, how much I still got hot for her smell, her skin, her smile.

Cause she was off limits.

Besides, she deserved someone better than me.

So I needed to put the thought of that kiss out of my mind and remember why the hell I went to so much trouble to stay away from her all those years.

Because I knew what it was like to unravel, to come unhinged, and I'd spent a long ass time pulling my shit together.

I was a grown man now with a killer job, and I knew better than to feel bad about things I once wanted and couldn't have.

And of all the things that qualified to be on that list, Jen was right at the top.

So it didn't matter if her skin was soft. It didn't matter if holding her face in my hands made me feel more right than anything ever had. And it didn't matter if kissing her made me feel sky high.

All that mattered was that she was my guest.

And it was about time I kept my hands to myself.

THIRTEEN
- Jenny -

I watched some kissing montages on my laptop after Ethan left.

I was hoping the sight of other people's passionate kisses might help me stop dwelling on ours.

It didn't work very well, though, so I stopped and went back to practicing my lines.

When I needed a break, I made myself one of the packets of Easy Mac I'd brought with me. I know I should've been braving the big city or at least not eating Easy Mac now that I was a college graduate, but it was so comforting and cheesy and delicious.

Kind of like movie kisses.

After I washed my bowl, I crossed to the door by the bookshelf again and turned the handle. It was still locked.

I was sure there was nothing interesting in there. It was probably gross lacrosse equipment or porno mags or DVDs or something, but the fact that it was locked unsettled me.

Like a mouse in a maze, I knew I'd feel more comfortable if I was able to sniff out every corner of my new habitat, but the locked door was standing in my way.

I tried to imagine what a person living alone needed a locked door for, but I couldn't think of anything.

And then the thought occurred to me that Ethan might have his very own red room of pain and the idea made me feel so completely uncomfortable that I had to talk myself down.

After all, chances were it was just crap.

Still, it must've been important crap or it wouldn't need to be kept under lock and key. Right?

What's more, it bothered me that I didn't know what could be so important to him when we were family.

Sort of. I mean, I knew we weren't close, but wouldn't Marsha have known what was in Greg's closet?

When I considered his room at our parent's house, it didn't help.

His space had virtually no personality. Then again, I suppose mine wouldn't have either if it were up to Ed. His days in the military made him a stickler for standards, especially in terms of a people's personal space.

I can still remember the fight he and my mom had after I asked if I could put a Twilight poster on my wall. In the end, it came down to one of those "I don't tell you how to raise your kid" moments.

But Ethan's room was completely bare apart from a few sports trophies and a desk with a picture of his mom on it. And apart from the latter, he never struck me as the sentimental type.

After all, if there had been so much as a passed note or a dirty magazine in his room, I would've found it. Cause not only was I desperate to know more about him, but I had lots of friends over the years that were, too, and I wasn't exactly difficult when they wanted to snoop through his personal space.

And his apartment was just as mysterious, largely on account of that damn door.

Later that night, I found myself glancing at the clock a lot, wondering what Ethan was doing at work.

I assumed he was a good bartender and being good at anything was an attractive quality. I wondered what kind of women flirted with him on the job and if they ever gave him tips that weren't strictly monetary.

I shuddered at the thought.

As luck would have it, I looked at the clock at eleven past eleven and, as always, I decided to make a wish.

But I was torn.

Part of me wanted to wish that things wouldn't be awkward after our kiss.

But I knew wishing away my own awkwardness was damn near impossible from personal experience.

As a result, I decided to wish for the role of Marilyn because at least then our kiss wouldn't have been in vain.

A second later, my phone rang.

I paused Catastrophe on my laptop before picking up. "Hi, Mom."

"Hi, Honey. How are you?"

"Fine. Good."

"What do you think of New York so far?"

I smiled. "The size is a little intimidating, but I love the buzz of the place."

"Oh good," she said. "And how did your audition go? It was today, wasn't it?"

"Yeah."

"I'm sorry I couldn't call sooner, I was covering for Margie tonight so-"

"That's okay. It went really well. They want me to come back in and audition for a speaking part."

"That's fantastic."

"I know. Way more than I was expecting."

"When's the callback?"

"Thursday."

"I'll keep my fingers crossed for you."

"Thanks." I pinched one of the buttons on my pajama top.

"How are you and Ethan getting along?"

I swallowed. "Okay."

"Just okay?"

I shrugged.

"Is he being moody?"

"No." I took a deep breath. "He's fine. But just so you know, Ed never told him I was coming, and I don't think Ethan ever gave him permission to copy his key. So he was kind of ticked at first."

Silence.

"Mom?"

"I didn't realize that was the situation. That must've been awkward for you."

"Yeah."

"Was Ethan really upset?"

I bit the inside of my cheek. "Honestly, I think he expects that kind of thing from Ed at this point. I wouldn't bring it up anyway."

"Mmm. I thought Ed was mellowing out, but maybe he's not quite as far along as I thought."

"Everything's fine otherwise. His place is really nice. He's… tidy."

"That's good to hear."

"And I probably won't have to cramp his style for much longer."

"I'm sure you're not cramping his style."

"I'm trying not to."

"Well, I'll call to check on you soon."

"Okay."

"Give Ethan a hug for me."

"Sure," I said.

As if I could stop at a hug.

FOURTEEN
- Ethan -

I liked working at the club early in the week.

It was a different crowd, an arguably cooler crowd than the hoards that nearly busted the door down to get in at the weekend.

I didn't know if it was because we got more freelance, hipster types in or what, but for some reason, the people that could party late on Monday and Tuesday seemed a more mellow bunch.

What's more, not only could I actually have some banter with my coworkers while we poured drinks, but people were less likely to be on drugs so I was able to carry on more interesting conversations with the customers.

Once Thursday night rolled around, though, it was too busy to think, much less chat. Most of the time I just shut my brain off and made drinks like a sexy robot would... the sexy part meaning I threw in the occasional wink or compliment depending on who was around.

After all, I wasn't just a bartender. I was a host. Or at least that's what my buddy Ben repeated until he was blue in the face when we first opened the doors.

I met him through Christophe, who used to be a regular at the last place I worked. I don't know how he and Ben met. I didn't understand how any rich people met. It just sort of happened, as if money had a distinct scent or something.

Anyway, he was the one that got me the job, and being head bartender at the most exclusive club in town had changed everything for me. I was earning more money than I could spend, meeting more women than I could fuck, and having more fun than I'd ever had.

I absolutely loved it.

How could I not?

After so many years of rules and regulations and uniforms and watching my language and being in control, it was a huge relief to be around people who were relaxed, people who were just trying to have a good time.

Sure, there were benefits to my strict education. I learned a bit of much needed respect, was able to look after myself, and had a level of personal discipline that was unparalleled... at least, when Jen wasn't around.

But becoming the person I was had a cost, and I'd spent more time feeling oppressed than I would wish on any man.

Still, I was free at last.

All that mattered now was that working in a room full of tipsy people made me forget the raps on the knuckles, the pushups in the mud, the please sir yes sirs I muttered every time I wanted to piss or shit or blow my goddamn nose.

Escaping that environment was all I thought about for years, and I'd done it. And it was just as amazing as I thought it would be.

And then Jen showed up.

Yes, she had a beautiful face, and yes, I was ashamed of how much I liked her laugh and her smell and her spunkiness.

But her presence was a downer, too.

Cause I felt like a success most of the time. But seeing her again reminded me that while I'd come a long way, there was much I hadn't achieved.

After all, there were only two things I ever really wanted so much it hurt, two things I was too chicken to go after.

Jen was one of them.

And the other, well, I didn't see how I was ever going to get that either.

But I couldn't shake the nagging feeling that those two things were only out of reach because I wasn't fucking reaching for them.

Was there something wrong with me? Did other people go around ignoring what they wanted most?

What kind of success did that really make me? After all the effort I put into becoming a man, I was still afraid to go after what I wanted.

What was I so afraid of?

That I'd pursue my goals and get rejected on both counts?

I didn't see how that would make much difference to my life.

Take Jenny, for example. We couldn't be friends. I was too attracted to her, too interested in her, too aware of how her body moved in space.

And we couldn't be proper siblings. We weren't related. Apart from the obligation I felt to look out for her, I didn't have a single other familial feeling about her.

So the question was, could we be more than friends? Do more than kiss?

Was that completely ridiculous?

Frankly, part of me hoped my gag reflex would kick in when I went to kiss her and make it impossible to go through with it.

But that hadn't happened. On the contrary, I had to restrain myself from the urge I felt to pull her hips against me and let her feel the effect her taste had on my body.

What if I'd taken it further?

Would she have stopped me?

Of course, there was a question I needed to ask before I even considered those.

And that question was, how wrong was it to want more with her?

I knew my dad wouldn't be impressed, but I hadn't impressed my dad since I graduated second in my class, and I didn't do that to impress him. I did that to prove to myself that I wasn't the piece of shit he thought I was.

And what could he even do if he found out I'd laid my hands on her?

Beat the shit out of me?

Maybe ten years ago, but he didn't even have all his original parts anymore. The chances of him raising a hand to me were slim. And it wouldn't matter anyway because no one was more interested in protecting Jen than I was.

Hell, I'd been protecting her my whole life.

The only problem was that no one else knew it, including her.

What's more, I didn't know if she wanted me like that, if she felt anything during that kiss. And while I was happy for other women to consider me a mistake, I didn't want her to look at me that way.

I liked how she looked at me now- with a mixture of curiosity and feigned disapproval, disapproval that I noticed she forgot to feign when I walked around my apartment shirtless.

Plus, I'd always wanted to believe that my coming into her life was no accident, but after all this time, I still didn't know what to make of her. Of us.

And something told me that if I didn't figure it out while she was here, I might never know, might never even see her again.

And that thought made my heart ache because I'd missed her more than I realized.

After all, she was my yellow daisies.

FIFTEEN
- Jenny -

I woke up Thursday morning in a pair of thick socks that didn't belong to me.

Yesterday, it was an extra blanket.

Either I looked really cold when I slept, or Ethan felt guilty about something. Perhaps it was the fact that he'd been curt with me ever since the kiss.

I figured there was something else on his mind, though, because I don't see how I could've offended him during our read through. After all, I kissed him back and didn't initiate anything more. I merely followed his lead.

And I would've done it again in a heartbeat.

But he didn't offer to help me practice again.

I don't know if he thought once was enough or if he felt weird about kissing me, but I was starting to think it was time to clear the air between us.

I pulled the thick socks off my feet, feeling relieved that I'd painted my toes a bright tangerine color before my trip out here. At least I could rest assured that my feet hadn't offended him- though I had no idea how he put them on without waking me…

Especially considering my audition was today, and I'd woken so many times in the night from nerves.

Of course, I must've slept deeply at some point because I kept dreaming I was the girl in The Notebook kissing Ryan Gosling in the rain over and over again.

Hopefully I wasn't making soft little groaning noises in my sleep whenever he got home. That would be embarrassing.

Speaking of sleepy noises, I could tell by the sound coming from under his door that he was still conked out.

Yesterday, I waited until he woke up naturally again and was bursting for the toilet by the time he stumbled shirtless out of his room.

I was starting to think that was actually his preferred level of dress and that he wasn't actually doing it to torture me.

Though it still did.

Why did the hottest guy I knew have to be my stepbrother?

Had I been a murdering bandit in a past life? A Spaniard with a blanket full of small pox? Judas himself?

I mean, I'd only kissed him once and already I knew I'd probably compare every man I ever met going forward to him no matter how hard I tried not to.

But it was more than that.

For instance, just watching him fold his laundry at the kitchen table made me feel like I was going to break out in a heat rash. I don't know if it was my fascination with his military precision or the fact that he was shirtless at the time, but being around him was overloading my senses.

I seriously needed a Xanax.

Not that I'd ever taken one, but isn't that how a professional actor would've coped with this situation?

Ugh.

Even the low laugh he let out when he was reluctant to find something funny made my stomach feel hollow in a way that only his mischievous smile could fill up.

It was fucked up.

And the kiss had only made it worse. Because for the first time since I tried to catch his eye on the bus at age fourteen, I actually felt like I had his full attention, and it was a high better than any drug.

Or so I imagined since my experience with drugs was very limited.

Sure, I'd puffed a few joints in college, but that didn't really count as drug use in my opinion.

And I did smoke cigs like a chimney sophomore year, but when I realized that I was only doing it because everyone else was and that it can make your boobs saggy, I packed it in after forty eight hours of extremely ticklish coughing fits.

The point is, I still remember when he got on that bus.

He was older than me. I probably shouldn't even have attempted to make eye contact with him, but I felt really great about myself that morning because the front of my backpack was full of perfectly sharpened number two pencils, brand new notebooks, and folders I really liked.

I hated when my mom left school shopping until the end of summer, and I was forced to choose the half a dozen folders that I found the least offensive.

But that summer- perhaps because she knew I was nervous about going to high school in the first place- she took me in July so I got my pick of the bunch.

I realize now that my level of excitement for pretty folders probably only enhanced the toxic eau de geek I gave off back then, a scent Ethan and his friends could probably pick up a mile away.

But I wasn't that unhappy when he didn't sit down next to me. I had this weird calm in my chest, as if I knew I would have a chance to get to meet him another time, as if I sensed that we were destined to know each other sooner or later.

And I was right. It just didn't happen the way I would've liked.

I took a deep breath outside his door and cracked it open.

On account of my audition, I couldn't wait for him to wake up. I needed to get in the bathroom to get ready.

He was sleeping face down, the top covers dangerously close to his butt, his solid back looking good enough to eat off of.

I raised one hand beside my face like a blinder and tiptoed like a cartoon cat towards the bathroom.

"Morning," he groaned.

"Morning," I whispered, hoping he would notice how respectful I was trying to be of his space.

He rolled onto his side and propped his head up with his hand.

I dropped my blinder and looked at him. His face was still soft and sleepy.

"I'm sorry if I woke you," I said. "I just have to get ready for my audition so-"

"It's fine. I have to get up anyway."

"Oh good," I said, prying my mind away from the question of whether he was naked under the covers. "Thanks for the socks by the way."

He scrunched his face. "The socks?"

"That you put on me last night when you got home?"

"Oh. Sure. Don't mention it."

I took another step towards the bathroom door.

He scooted up and leaned against his navy blue pillows. "You nervous about today?"

I shrugged. "A healthy amount. Or so I'm telling myself."

He nodded and yawned. "I'm sure you'll do great."

I raised my eyebrows. "Yeah?" Kind words from him were like puddles in the desert- too few and far between to ignore.

"Somebody has to get the part, right? Might as well be you."

"Thanks." I reached for the bathroom doorknob, trying to keep my eyes from scouring his chest.

"Just kiss him the way you kissed me and you'll definitely get the part."

I forced a smile and closed myself in the bathroom.

What the fuck was that supposed to mean?

"Hey Jen?"

"Yeah?" I called through the door.

"Don't lock the door. I gotta take a piss, but I'll wait until you get in the shower."

My eyes grew wide. "Great," I said. Absolutely freaking fantastic.

SIXTEEN
- Ethan -

I did have to piss, but I could've waited. I didn't need to go in there when I knew she was naked and soaping herself up on the other side of my city skyline shower curtain.

I guess I did it just to torture myself.

Though the flush was to torture her.

And when she called me an asshole, I felt like I was back on track. After all, the more she pushed me away, the sooner she'd stop feeling like the carrot at the end of my fucking stick.

Besides, I had to do something after she called me out for giving her my best socks. Why did she have to mention it?

And why did she have to kiss some theatre tit to get a part?

That thought alone was completely ruining my day.

In fact, I found it so upsetting that I threw on a hoodie and headed to MoMA to distract myself.

It was one of my favorite places.

Where I was from, there were no museums, no interesting sculptures, and nowhere that didn't smell like farm.

Hell, the closest I ever got to any culture as a kid was the Ohio State Fair, and there are only so many times a person can get excited about seeing a life size cow made of butter.

But MoMA was exciting every time.

I even met a woman at the club once who invited me to see some of the older pieces in the archived collection that was down in the basement and no longer on public display. She showed me some new stuff while we were down there, too, but that's a story for another day.

A day when I'm not trying to avoid the thought of rough, inappropriate sex.

Of course, museums are pretty sexy places.

Sure, modern art was a bit hit and miss, but it was the hits I was after.

Every now and then I'd come across something with such surprising colors or shapes that I could admire it for ages, seeing something new in it every few seconds. I liked the modern stuff because it raised questions, whereas more classic art seemed to be about providing answers.

But that was just my take. I suppose the whole point is that it's subjective, that it reflects more about the viewer than the artists themselves... Unless we're talking Frida Kahlo's work in which case that is some straight autobiographical craziness.

The other thing I liked about the museum was that it was a place for quiet contemplation. Like church, but without the forced religious undertones.

I remember seeing Ferris Bueller's Day Off as a kid and watching that part where Ferris and his friends stand in front of paintings at the Art Institute of Chicago.

At one point, his buddy Cameron studies Seurat's *Day in the Park*, and his eyes zoom in on the pointillism, his focus on fewer dots in every shot.

That's how I felt as a teenager the first time I noticed the freckles on Jen's nose. Like Seurat wishes he'd painted something so interesting.

But I'd always liked things that could be appreciated from different angles, different distances. And I liked modern art because it wasn't the kind of art I made so I could just enjoy it without feeling the need to compare it to my own work.

I was admiring the use of color in Matisse's *The Parakeet and the Mermaid* when my phone started buzzing against my thigh.

I pulled it out, silenced it, and slid it back in my pocket. A moment later, it buzzed again. I did the same.

However, I knew from experience it was going to go off again so I kept it in my hand and headed for the doors to the courtyard.

"Hello," I said, after it started ringing for the third time.

"What took you so long?" my dad asked in an accusatory tone that I doubted was good for his blood pressure.

"I was helping an old lady across the street." I could practically hear him rolling his eyes. However, he was so tangibly obsessed with my becoming a contributing member of society when I was younger that I couldn't help but find jokes about what a Good Samaritan I'd become hugely entertaining.

It was also the only thing he couldn't argue with, which was exciting since my dad was the kind of guy who could start an argument with the mirror.

"Where are you really?"

"At the art museum," I said. "Helping the handicapped people get up the ramp."

"Last try."

"Ringing my Salvation Army bell outside the supermarket."

"Why do you insist on spewing such crap when you know I have no sense of humor?"

"Because of the lifelong pledge I took to help you loosen up."

He groaned.

"Yeah, yeah. I know it hasn't been working, but I consulted the experts and they think prune juice might help."

"Is that a constipation joke?"

I smiled. "See? We're making progress after all."

"How's your sister?"

"I don't have a sister."

"You know what I mean. Jen. How is she?"

"Well, it's hard to say because I don't really know how she normally is?"

"Normally she's bubbly and smiling and occasionally singing to herself."

"I'd say she's herself, then, minus the singing, but perhaps she's just shy around people who aren't tone deaf."

"I'm not tone deaf."

"Whatever you say."

"So she's fine?"

"Yeah." I yanked on the strings of my hoodie. "She's at her audition right now."

"Oh good. I hope it goes well. She really deserves a break."

I furrowed my brow. "Can you put my dad back on the phone?"

"What?"

"What happened to Mr. What-Doesn't-Kill-You-Ma-"

"She's strong enough already."

I rolled my eyes at the way he said it- like he was the fucking authority on strength.

"Besides, she's put up with a lot of my shit over the years, and it would be nice if someone else recognized how special she is."

"Have you gone soft?"

"No."

Maybe she'd just melted him? Like she melted everyone else around her, myself included.

"I just know how bad she wants this and she's delicate, you know? I don't want her to have any setbacks, and I know what an unforgiving industry it is that she's trying to break into."

"How? From all your days tap dancing with Hugh Jackman?"

"You know what I mean."

"I'm not sure I do."

"Fine. Be dense. Just look after her, okay? She's not used to being a small fish in such a massive pond."

"Right."

"She's trusting and naive and her street smarts are no better than an earthworm's."

"Something tells me she wouldn't appreciate that."

"All I'm saying is that I've seen her cry, and it isn't pretty."

"Why would she be crying?"

"Just look after her, okay?"

"I am. What the hell? As if I had a choice after the way she just showed up." I flinched. I didn't want to give him the satisfaction of knowing he got one over on me.

"Sorry about that."

"About what? Getting a copy of my key cut without asking?"

"Yeah."

"Apology not accepted." I shook my head. "Who the fuck do you think you are anyway?"

"A concerned parent."

"Concerned isn't the word that comes to my mind."

"I said I was sorry, okay? That's the best I can do. Old habits and all that."

"That's no excuse," I said. "You invaded my privacy and then invited Jen to impose on me. Did it ever occur to you how uncomfortable that must've been for her?"

"No."

I sighed. "Well, I've done my best to make her feel welcome, but the guise you sent her here under didn't help things."

"Mmm."

"And I get that the Golden Rule wasn't a big part of your army training, but you might want to look it up."

"I take your point."

"Good."

"Have a nice day," he said. "And tell Jenny I said hi."

"Yeah. Sure."

Love you, too.

SEVENTEEN
- Jenny -

I couldn't believe it.

After all that fuss, I didn't even have to do the kissing scene.

To say I was relieved didn't even begin to cover it.

And I channeled that relief into the adrenaline I was already feeling and totally nailed my audition. At least, it felt like I did.

And when the director said he wanted to have a word in his office, I was feeling even more confident.

After all, if he thought I was a nobody going nowhere, he wouldn't have gone out of his way to give me individual attention, right?

Why would he? I mean, I knew enough to know that show business wasn't about letting people down easy and handing out attaboys.

Of course, after forty five minutes of lying low in the back of the theater and watching the people who came in to audition after me, I started to have my doubts.

Some of my competition was really professional. And they stuck out like crazy, dancing through their auditions like it wasn't even the only one they had that day. Like they were merely doing the director a favor by coming in, which was both sort of inspiring and completely unendearing.

However, there were others whose visible nerves made my heart break for them. One girl was sick and couldn't sing the song she was supposed to. Another boy was so nervous he couldn't stop stuttering.

It made me question how I came across.

Frankly, I feel like anyone with experience would've been able to tell that this was my first rodeo, but Brandi often told me that I gave off an unapproachable aloof vibe when I was nervous.

Whatever. It didn't matter.

All that mattered was that the director wanted to see me in his office, so I arrived perfectly on time, well aware that every second his eyes were on me was another chance to impress.

I took a deep breath and knocked on the wooden door.

"Who's there?"

I turned the doorknob and poked my head in. "You wanted to see me, Mr. Leighton?"

He looked up from behind a heavy looking black desk. "Jennifer, yes. Come in."

I stepped in his office and tried to act less nervous than I felt, which was a role I was growing more accustomed to all the time.

He stood up and gestured towards the chair in front of his desk. "Please, have a seat."

I did as he asked, noticing that he looked less intimidating in the small office than he did in the front row when I was on stage.

He sat back down and smiled. "And please call me Ken."

"Sure," I said, doing a cartwheel inside that I was on a first name basis was a real big time casting director.

"Tell me a little bit about yourself, Jennifer." He leaned back in his chair. He was wearing a black V-neck shirt that clung to him like his matching gelled hair.

I pursed my lips. "Well, I'm from a small town in Ohio, and I studied acting at Oberlin."

"Your family must be very proud of you."

I nodded.

"I bet they'd be even more proud if you got a leading role in this production right out of school."

"Of course," I said. "They already told me they'd come see me in it and everything."

"That's fantastic." I felt his eyes dip below mine and pulled the front of my tank top up automatically.

"I take it you liked my audition?" I asked.

He lined up the fingers on his hands and looked at me. "I was very impressed, yes. Especially by the energy you brought to the role. I like each of my cast members to treat their part like it's the biggest one in the production so no one gets out acted by their peers, and I really think you can bring the right intensity to the role of Marilyn."

I raised my eyebrows.

"In fact, your audition was so good it's put me in a bit of a pickle."

I tilted an ear towards him. "How's that?"

"Can I be honest with you?"

"Of course."

"There are two other young women up for the same part."

I swallowed.

"One of them has a lot more experience than you, and she's already proven that she has the stamina to deliver night after night."

"Uh-huh."

"And the other woman looks a lot more like the real Marilyn did, and while I hate to be swayed by something so superficial, I know from experience that when the physical resemblance is there, it's one less thing the audience has to overcome to really get into the performance."

I slid my sweaty palms down my thighs as covertly as I could.

Ken stood up, walked around his desk, and leaned against it. He came so close I had to lean my head back to keep my eyes on his.

"So it really comes down to what I'm looking for," he said.

"And what's that?"

"Well, some of the things I'm looking for are obvious enough- dedication, sex appeal, someone with a youthful energy who can convincingly convey the spirit of the free loving sixties."

"Sure."

He wrapped his hands around the edge of the desk. "But there are other things I can't tell as well from a traditional audition."

"Like what?" I asked, doing my best to ignore the bulge in his black jeans.

"Like how well someone takes direction," he said, moving his feet a little farther apart.

"For what it's worth, I've always felt that was one of my strengths," I said, scooting back in my chair in the hopes that the air might feel less thin there.

"And how bad do you want the part, Jennifer?"

He was officially leering at me. At first I had my doubts and didn't want to believe it, but the way he was looking at me no longer felt supportive or good. "I wouldn't be here if I didn't want it."

He nodded, a smarmy smile spreading across his face. "Of course. I suppose that's a silly question.

I felt my pulse quicken in my tightening chest. Something wasn't right. The air, the room, the look on his face. It all felt strangely sinister all of a sudden.

"Allow me to let you in on two little secrets," he said, lowering his voice.

"Okay."

"It's all who you know."

I swallowed. "So I've heard."

He raised his eyebrows. "You want to know the second secret?"

I nodded.

"The people who make it in this business- the people you look up to- they made their own luck from the beginning."

I furrowed my brow. "What are you saying?"

He stepped up to me and lifted my chin with his fingertips.

My blood ran cold at his touch.

"I'm saying that, as far as I'm concerned, there's only one thing standing between you and a standing ovation on opening night."

"I'm not sure what you're getting at," I said, shrinking in my chair.

"Let me spell it out for you," he said, pulling down his zipper. "You do me a favor, and I do you one."

My stomach wretched as he tucked a wisp of hair behind my ear.

"So what'll it be, Miss Layne? Are you ready to be a star?"

EIGHTEEN
- Ethan -

I dropped the garbage bag full of linoleum cuttings into the dumpster and headed back upstairs to get cleaned up.

When I walked in the door, I had two missed calls.

I hit redial and waited.

She didn't pick up.

I tried again.

"Ethan?"

Jen's voice sounded weird. It was the same tone I'd expect someone to use if their phone rang while they were hiding in the Hunger Games arena.

"How did your audition go?"

"I- don't- know," she said, gasping between every word.

"Are you okay?"

"I- don't- know-"

"Are you hurt?"

"No. No-"

"Where are you?"

"I- don't-"

Every hair on my body went stiff as I imagined the worst. "Breathe dammit and tell me where you are!" Despite my dad's overdramatic fear mongering, this was New York, and there was truth to his concerns. This city was full of gutters big enough for a girl like Jen and worse. So much worse.

"I'm-I'm-"

"Find a street sign or something. Anything. Describe where you are." I wrapped my fist around my keys and pressed the phone to my ear.

"I'm outside a hotel," she stuttered. "The Abbott Hotel."

My chest loosened instantly. "Okay, I need you to listen to me carefully."

"Uh-huh."

"Go in the hotel. There will be a bunch of comfy chairs right in the front room. Sit down and wait for me to get there."

"Okay."

"And if you need anything, there's a man behind the desk named Paul. He knows me."

"Are you sure?"

"Yes. You're safe there. I promise. I'll be there as soon as I can."

"Thanks," she whispered.

My heart felt like it was going to pound right through my shirt. Fuck. What the hell happened? She was fine when she left? Had she been jumped? Assaulted? Hit by a car? It could be anything and she'd given me nothing.

Waiting for the elevator was killing me. I pulled out my phone and dialed Ben.

"What's up, buddy?"

"Hey-you at the hotel."

"Not today, I'm-"

"Is Ella there?"

"Probably," he said. "Why?"

"My stepsister just called me from there and she's hysterical-"

"I didn't know you had a sister."

"She's not my fucking sister."

"Okay, Ethan. Whoa. Just relax, man. Is she alright?"

"I don't know. I'm on my way there now." The elevator dinged and I got on. "I just thought if someone was there to make sure she's okay-"

"Sure. Leave it with me."

"Yeah?"

"If I can't get ahold of Ella, I'll go myself. I'm only a few blocks away."

"I owe you one, Boss."

"Nonsense," he said. "I'll do what I can."

I hung up and bounced on the balls of my feet like I was warming up for a fight, springing out of the elevator as soon as I could. I felt some relief at the fact that she was at the Abbott, but not knowing why she sounded so weird was making me sick.

I unlocked my jeep as soon as I got close and slid into the driver's seat, reversing out of my spot out before I'd even closed the door.

I should've fucking taken her to the audition myself.

What the hell else was I doing? Milling around the museum? I could do that every day of the week. Hell, sometimes I did.

Would it have killed me to go out of my way for her?

Sure, she gave me the vibe that she wanted to be treated like an independent woman, but I knew she was more vulnerable than she realized. I never should've let her out of my fucking sight.

It might've been a bit overbearing, but she was used to my dad for Christ's sake. And at least then I wouldn't be in this situation, wondering if she was okay while I wasn't by her side.

Forget being a lousy stepbrother. I wasn't even being a decent friend.

She deserved better.

And who was I kidding?

I didn't need to push her away. She was going places. Big places. I'd be lucky if she even remembered my fucking name. Who the hell did I think I was? As if a girl like Jen might get so attached to being around me she wouldn't leave.

I wasn't that good of a kisser.

Besides, she was only staying with me because it was convenient. If she had two pennies to rub together, not only would she have stayed somewhere else, but she probably wouldn't have even called to say she was in the city.

After all, it's not like we were close.

Which somehow made it even worse that I hadn't been a better host.

When I came to a red light, I let my head fall against the headrest and dropped my hands in my lap, revealing the streak of blue paint I'd inadvertently transferred onto the steering wheel with my vice grip.

"Fuck."

I rubbed the spot with my thumb, but it was no use. Then I grabbed a napkin out of the side door and scrubbed the side of my hand, stopping a second later when I realized dry paint particles were probably just as deadly to my black leather interior.

As soon as the light changed, I sped ahead, weaving in and out of cars and getting beeped at even more than I was used to. When I saw the flags over the hotel up ahead, I felt a surge of adrenaline.

All I could think about was seeing her.

All I wanted was to know she was okay.

Even if she couldn't forgive me for letting her go alone, I prayed that she'd at least be okay enough that I could live with myself.

I pulled the car up outside the hotel, grateful that the valet on duty was a guy I recognized.

"I won't be long," I said, handing him my keys and a folded bill. "Just picking someone up."

I ran through the front doors and scanned the room like a bear on his hind legs.

And then I saw her.

She was sitting on a small crème colored couch with Ella.

I headed in their direction.

They saw me at the same time.

The first thing I noticed was the marks around Jen's eyes, but as I got closer, I was relieved to see it was only smeared mascara. My eyes bounced around the rest of her body, searching for any obvious signs of struggle or injury.

That's when I noticed she was holding Ella's hand.

Ella stood up when I reached them. "Hi Ethan," she said, leaning in and pressing her cheek to mine. "Can I have a quick word?"

"Are you okay?" I said, squatting down in front of Jen. Her eyes were as red as her lips.

She nodded.

"Ethan," Ella said.

"I'll be right here," I said to Jen.

She blinked.

I put a hand on her cheek and took in her face one last time before standing up.

"Thanks for waiting with her," I said to Ella once we'd walked a few feet away.

"Of course," she said. "I'm sorry I couldn't do more to help."

I furrowed my brow. "Do you know what happened?"

She shook her head. "No. She couldn't say- or didn't want to. Who knows? I can't blame her. It's not like she knows me."

I craned my neck forward. "She didn't tell you anything?"

Ella shrugged. "Only that she isn't physically hurt."

NINETEEN
- Jenny -

I was so relieved when he walked in.

Sure, I was embarrassed that I'd called him in hysterics.

But when he came through those doors, I felt like I could finally let out the breath I'd been holding since he promised he'd come.

I didn't move while he talked to Ella.

I just sat on the couch, happy to be around people who seemed to genuinely have my best interests in mind. I could feel Ethan looking over Ella's shoulder at me as they spoke in hushed tones a few feet away.

Apparently, her husband owned this place, and his son was Ethan's boss.

That was all news to me. Everything she said was, and once she realized I wasn't in the mood to do much talking, she just took over, chatting away as if it were the most normal thing in the world to babysit a strange woman in your husband's hotel.

She mostly talked about how she knew Ethan and what a good bartender he was.

She also made me promise that if we ever went to karaoke that I would make him sing an Elvis song. She said he didn't sing anything like Elvis, but apparently he'd perfected the moves and was guaranteed to bring the house down.

It was strange to hear a complete stranger say they'd seen him be silly. I'd never seen him do a silly thing in my life. On the contrary, he always seemed so serious it made me feel giddy in comparison, and if the face he'd been making since he walked in the hotel was anything to go by, he wasn't about to bust out his hilarious.

Regardless, I needed to get a grip. I'd obviously blown my cover as a competent woman about town, inconveniencing Ethan's friends to make matters worse.

Fortunately, I was pretty exhausted from the emotional breakdown I had after I left the studio, not to mention the hour I walked in circles after my bleary eyes caused me to lose my way. But I was actually feeling much better now- or not necessarily better, but tired. And safe at last.

"Come on," Ethan said, extending a hand in front of me.

"You guys can hang out as long as you want," Ella said. "Or if you'd rather have some privacy-"

"It's fine," Ethan said. "You've done enough, thanks."

"Sure." She extended a pack of tissues in my direction. "It was nice to meet you, Jen."

I took them and smiled at her. She was so pretty. Like a real princess. "Thanks. You, too."

"I hope to see you again under more pleasant circumstances."

I nodded and took Ethan's hand, relishing the wave of warmth that coursed through my body as I stood up. I watched Ella walk away. When I turned back to Ethan, he was staring at me, his eyes dark and intense.

"What happened?" he asked. "You had me worried sick."

"I'm sorry." I cast my eyes down. "I just got a bit upset and then I got lost, and I know I shouldn't have bothered you, but-"

"Yes, you should've," he said, ducking his head to catch my eye. "And a lot sooner by the sound of it."

He couldn't have known how right he was.

"You happy to get out of here?" he asked.

I nodded.

He reached around and set his hand on my lower back.

It felt like an anchor that made the world around me stop spinning.

As my feet moved across the floor, I hoped people weren't giving him funny looks. After all, it wasn't his fault I was a hot mess.

When we got outside, he took his keys from the valet, walked over to the curbside Range Rover, and opened the door for me.

I thanked him with my eyes before climbing in and watching him walk around the front of the car.

After he got in, he just sat there for a second. The air in the car was heavy between us, as if we were the only still things in the whole city.

"I'm sorry I didn't take you to your audition," he said. "I should have offered. I wasn't thinking-"

"Don't blame yourself."

He laughed. "I don't want to, but until I know what the hell happened, I can't help but feel like this is all my faul-"

"It's not."

"Did something happen at the audition?"

A horn sounded behind us and he scowled in the rearview mirror before pulling out into traffic.

"You could say that."

"Did it not go well?"

I sighed.

"Well?"

I looked out my window. "I blew it."

He pulled up behind a convertible and flicked his turn signal on. "Are you sure?"

"Oh, I'm definitely sure."

"How did you blow it?" he asked. "Was it the kiss?"

I turned and looked at him, my eyes dropping to his lips. A warm shiver shot up my neck. "No."

He exhaled, his broad shoulders dropping.

"I didn't have to do it."

Half his mouth curled up into a smile.

"What the hell's so funny?"

"Nothing," he said. "It's just nice that you didn't have to kiss anyone if you weren't going to get the part anyway."

I rolled my eyes. "Yeah. Real nice."

"Any chance you'll get a smaller part?"

I looked out the windshield again. "Zero chance. In fact, I might never get work in this town at all."

He laughed.

I glared at him.

"Sorry. I assumed you were being dramatic."

"I wish."

"Are you hungry?"

I looked at him, searching his face for clues as to whether he was still joking around. "You're serious?"

He shrugged. "I'm kind of hungry."

I let my head fall back against the headrest.

"But if you're too upset to watch me eat-"

"I could use a drink."

He raised his eyebrows. "Yeah?"

"Is that so hard to believe?"

"No," he said. "Can I take you somewhere for one or would you rather pick up some Mike's Hard and go back to my place?"

"I don't drink that shit anymore."

"Thank god."

"Just like I assume you don't drink Ice House anymore."

He laughed. "Not even if it's on special."

I folded my arms. "You know I'm not the sissy teenager I was when you left, right?"

"And I'm not the adorable rogue you fell for on the bus the first day you saw me."

I swung my head around and narrowed my eyes at him. "What did you just say?"

"Or am I?"

"If you're suggesting-"

"What?" he asked, turning the car into a parking garage.

A smudge of blue paint on the wheel caught my eye. "Nothing," I said. "You're just trying to get a rise out of me, and I've had a shitty enough day as it is."

"I'm not after a rise," he said, taking a ticket and waiting for the striped bar to go up. "To be honest, I'd settle for the truth."

I groaned and slouched in my seat. "How about you drive and I drink?"

"Fine," he said. "Save it for your diary."

TWENTY
- Ethan -

I never got to see much of Jen's teenage dramatics so seeing her in a strop was kind of amusing for me.

However, not knowing what happened was still bothering me, and I was getting sick of pretending she didn't have to tell me. After all, if it was something fucking stupid, I'd know to stay calmer next time.

"Ella's nice," she said, reaching for a loaded potato skin.

I watched her dunk it in a pile of ketchup and scrunched my face.

"What?"

"Ketchup?" I asked. "On a potato skin?"

She craned her neck back and looked at the part she had left. "What? It's basically a French fry. Just in a different shape."

I leaned back in the booth and lifted my beer. As I took a sip, the Texas longhorn skull on the wall overhead edged into my peripheral vision.

"Don't you think?" she asked, stirring her comically large margarita with the lime slice poking out of it. "About Ella?"

"Yeah, she's great," I said. "Why?"

"Are all the girls who come to the club like her?"

I shook my head. "No. Not even close."

"She said you're more than a regular bartender."

I raised my eyebrows.

"Which explains your whip."

I squinted at her. "Sorry?"

She lifted her margarita with two hands, took a sip long enough to make the effort worthwhile, and set it back down. "Your car," she said, licking the salt off her lips.

"I know what a whip is."

"Oh," she said. "Well, it's nice."

"For a bartender, you mean."

"For anybody."

"Thanks," I said, taking a potato skin from my side of the plate.

"Whereas your place is so small-"

"This is New York."

"I know but-"

"But what?" I asked. "Your invisible place is way bigger?"

"Touché."

"So when are you going to tell me what happened?"

Her eyes fell to the plate between us as she reached for the last potato skin.

I slid the plate away. "Come on."

"That one's mine," she said. "You already had your four."

I craned my neck forward. "Yeah, I did. And I drove halfway across town to pick you up cause you'd cried yourself blind, so if you don't tell me what happened-"

She rolled her shoulders back and cocked her head. "What? You're going to eat my last potato skin?"

Perhaps I hadn't thought my bargaining chip through.

"You can have it," she said.

I groaned and slid the plate back towards her. "I don't want it. I just want to know what happened today."

"I already told you," she said. "I blew my audition."

"And that's why you were so upset?"

She nodded.

"So much for your thick skin."

"So much for thinking you weren't as big of an asshole as I thought."

"Did you sing out of tune or something?"

"No."

"Jen."

She raised her eyebrows.

"I'm not going to let this go."

She sighed. "If I tell you, do you promise not to make a big deal out of it?"

I laughed. "I'm sure you made a big enough deal out of it for both of us."

She clenched her jaw. Then she drained half of what was left in her trough of tequila.

"Sorry. I don't mean to make light of it. I know today was important to you."

She looked at me, her eyes glassy. "Promise."

"Sure, whatever. I promise."

"Promise you won't make a big deal out of it."

"Christ. I promise I won't make a big deal out of the big fucking deal, okay?"

She leaned back on her side of the wooden booth and crossed her arms.

I took a sip of my beer.

"After my audition, the casting director said he wanted to see me in his office."

"Uh-huh."

"He's the guy that gets to decide who gets what part."

"Got it."

"Promise you won't tell your dad either."

"No problem. I haven't told him anything since I was thirteen."

She stuck her lower lip out and considered the obvious truth I'd just told her.

"Go on."

"So at first things were going really well. He told me I had a lot of potential, and that he thought I could bring a lot of energy to the part."

"That's good."

"But then things took a weird turn, and he started saying how it's all who you know and that all the big stars make their own luck."

I nodded.

"And then he touched me." Her voice fell several decibels. "And he said the only thing standing in between me and getting the part was…"

"What?"

She glanced down, nodding her head towards her lap.

I craned my neck forward.

"You know." She swallowed and nodded at her lap again.

I shook my head. "No, I don't know."

"He wanted me to-" She gestured towards her lap.

I felt the back of my neck burst into flames.

She kept her eyes on mine.

I could tell by the sadness in her eyes that she was telling the truth. "He asked you to do that?"

She pursed her lips. "Not in so many words, but-"

I put my elbows on the table and slid my fingers in my hair as the sound of my heartbeat pounded in my ears. I'd only ever been this angry once, and it led to me getting expelled from school.

I took a deep breath, clenched my jaw, and exhaled through my nose.

Could I have heard her wrong?

Could some middle aged skid mark have seriously assaulted her this afternoon? Sexually? At a fucking job interview?

I kept my head down and pushed against the edge of the table, squeezing my hands around it until my knuckles turned white.

Christophe. I had to talk to Christophe. He would know what to do. He was always fucking saying that if shitheads only got legal advice before they took things into their own hands, they would make better choices.

And I needed some serious legal counseling, because for the first time in almost ten years, I really wanted to hurt somebody.

And hurt wasn't really the word. Maim was more like it.

I'd pound my fist into that guys face until his jaw had to be wired shut so tight he'd never so much as compliment another woman in his life.

"Ethan?"

I looked up at her, but it only made my anger worse.

Her face was so open, so youthful, so trusting. Only a real piece of shit would look at that face and have an opportunistic, dirty ass thought like that.

And anyone who would have that kind of thought deserved to suffer the kind of brain damage that would keep it from ever happening again.

"Are you okay?" she asked.

How was she not more upset? How could she sit there like nothing even happened when I felt like my blood pressure was going to make me burst out of my own skin?

And then I had a horrible sinking feeling. "Wait."

She raised her eyebrows. "What?"

"When you say you blew it-"

TWENTY ONE
- Jenny -

My mouth fell open.

He closed his.

I leaned across the table. "Are you fucking asking me what I think you're asking me?"

He lifted his palms in my direction. "I don't know. Do I need to?"

"Do you even know me at all?!"

He raised his eyebrows. "I know you as well as you know me."

I swallowed.

"Shit, Jen. You've gone to college since the last time I spent any time with you."

I shook my head.

"How am I supposed to know what your fucking values are?"

"Don't look at me like that."

"Like what?"

"Like you still don't know whether I'd do something like that. For a fucking part."

"Is that a no?"

I furrowed my brow. "Of course it is."

"No what?"

"No, I didn't literally blow it."

He exhaled and leaned back, pulling the collar of his hoodie away from the back of his neck.

"Jackass."

"Sorry. I had to ask."

I rolled my eyes. "Did you? Cause if I had, we'd be celebrating the fact that I'd scored a leading role in an Off Broadway production."

He shook his head. "No. If you'd obliged that asshole, we wouldn't have shit to celebrate."

"Really?"

He threw his hands in the air. "Are you second guessing yourself now?"

I tore a corner off my paper coaster. "No, I just-"

"Just what?"

"What if I missed my chance?"

He blinked at me.

"I mean, this guy could ruin my career before it even gets started."

"Sounds to me like he tried to do just that this afternoon."

"You know what I mean."

"No. I don't."

I sighed.

He slid the empty plate to the edge of the table and reached across it, putting his hand over mine. "Jen."

I stared at the place where he'd made my hand disappear. "What?"

"Look at me."

I raised my eyes to meet his.

"I'm proud of you," he said. "You did the right thing."

"I hope you'll be proud of me when I spend the next thirty years waiting tables."

"Come on," he said, squeezing my hand. "You don't mean that."

"I know, but it just felt like I was so close, ya know?"

"Hey. You think Jennifer Lawrence got where she is sucking dick?"

I flinched.

"You think Julia Roberts would ever even dream of dropping to her knees to impress a producer?"

"No."

"You think Meryl Streep would've done anything besides kick that prick in the balls?"

I smiled. "I suppose not."

"And you know who else is going to make it on talent alone?"

I raised my eyebrows. "Who?"

"Jennifer Layne," he said. "You're going to be one of those classy actresses that women want to be and men want to be with."

I turned an ear towards him. "Are you saying you want to be with Meryl?"

"Can you keep a secret?"

My heart pinched at the warm creases around his eyes. "Of course."

"I already have."

"Is that so?"

"And she might be the finest actress on the planet, but I assure you, she didn't have to fake her orgasm with me."

I pushed his hand away. "Jesus. Ethan!"

He leaned back and smiled.

"It's not okay to talk about Meryl like that."

"If you think that's bad, you should hear the kind of stuff she says about me."

"You wish."

He laughed, the low rumble echoing through my bones.

"Thanks," I said. "For saying that stuff before."

"It's true. You must know you did the right thing."

I nodded. "I do, yeah, but I still wish it hadn't happened."

"If you regret what didn't go down, just think how much you'd regret if something did."

"I know," I said, a chill running up my spine. "Plus, what if I'd gone through with it, and I still didn't get the part?"

His eyes grew wide.

"That was a joke," I said. "I don't even want to think about that."

"Me neither." He wrapped his hand around his beer and drained the rest of it. "I'm sorry I made light of you being upset before-"

I shook my head. "You didn't. You were great. You rescued me as soon as I told you I needed rescuing."

"I shouldn't have let you get in a situation where you needed to be rescued."

"It's not your job to protect me."

"About that-" He leaned forward and put his elbows on the table.

I raised my eyebrows. "What?"

"You know I have to kill this guy, right?"

"He's not worth the jail time."

"At the very least, I have to beat the shit out of him. It's only right."

"I don't want anything to do with you breaking your streak of peacefulness."

"I'm not doing it for you. I'm doing it for me."

I shook my head. "To quote one of my favorite movies, 'If might is right, then love has-'"

"No place in the world."

I furrowed my brow. "You know The Mission?"

He shrugged. "Of course. It's a classic."

I raised my eyebrows. "Then you'll recall that it's a movie about forgiveness."

"It's a movie about a lot of things, and that's just one of them."

I lifted my glass and licked a patch of salt off the rim before downing the last gulp.

"What's his name?"

"I'm not telling you."

"You think I can't find out? I know the name of the play and everything."

"You promised not to make a big deal about it."

"And I'm going to keep that promise," he said. "By not taking it to a homicidal level."

I cocked my head at him.

He raised his eyebrows.

"It means a lot to me that you're mad."

"Livid," he corrected. "Like about to give the Hulk a run for his money livid."

"Whatever kind of livid you are," I said. "Take it out on your next run."

He scrunched his face.

"Because I'm flattered that you want to protect me, but-"

"Actually, I think you do a pretty good job of protecting yourself."

I smiled.

"I just feel obligated to seek revenge on your behalf."

I lifted a palm in the air between us and spoke like a wizard. "I absolve you of your quest for revenge."

"Fine," he said. "Make me do it the hard way."

I leaned my neck forward. "Please don't find this guy. What if someone found out it was because of me? Then I'd be even more fucked than I am now."

"There's only one person that's getting fucked here, and he asked for it."

A flair covered waitress appeared at my side with another giant margarita.

I shook my head. "Oh- I didn't order another one."

She smiled and spoke with an affected Texas accent. "You don't have to, Hun. It's Thirsty Thursday. They're bottomless."

Ethan stuck his lower lip out and looked between my drink and the waitress. "In that case, would you mind bringing another one out?"

"Sure thing sugar lips."

And as he smiled back at her, I couldn't help but think she didn't know the half of it.

TWENTY TWO
- Ethan -

Her cheeks were pink by the time she finished her second margarita.

But that was two hours ago and even I'd lost track of how much we'd had.

"What time are you supposed to go to work?" she asked, laying a flat hand on the table.

I lifted my ass and pulled my phone from my pocket. "Fuck."

She raised her eyebrows. "Uh-oh."

"Hold on a second." I slipped out of the booth and headed towards the beer garden for some fresh air.

Ben answered on the second ring.

"Ethan- hey. I heard you got your sister okay."

"Stepsister," I said, leaning against an empty picnic table. "And yeah. I owe you one."

"Ella and Christophe's story don't really match up."

"What?"

"You told Christophe that she was bald and gay?"

I laughed. "If he'd expressed interest in Carrie, wouldn't you have done the same?"

"Have you been drinking?"

I scrunched my face. "I can't make it in tonight."

"What the fuck, man? I do you a favor and then you don't show up for work?"

"It's a long story. She was really upset and-"

"Yeah, Ella told me," he said. "What the hell happened?"

"She got assaulted."

"Seriously?"

"Yeah. On her fourth fucking day in the big city."

"That's rough. She okay?"

I nodded. "She is now that I've ploughed her full of margaritas."

"Good."

"And as pathetic as it is, I figured if I had a few, it might soften my urge to go paralyze the fucker."

"Good call," he said. "You're useless to me in prison."

"Can you manage tonight without me?"

"Yeah. Gretchen will be delighted to fill your shoes."

"Just as long as she doesn't get too comfortable in them."

"Don't worry. You're indispensable."

I smiled.

"Which is the only reason I'm putting up this shit."

"Oh come on. I've never done this before."

"I know, and I get it. If someone so much as leered at a hair on Carrie's head I'd-"

"What? Have them followed?"

"Shut the fuck up."

"I love you, Ben."

He laughed. "You're a twat. Enjoy the rest of the night. I'm glad your sister's okay."

"Stepsister," I said, but he'd already hung up.

I slid the phone back in my pocket, trying not to dwell on how crazy it was that I'd been having so much fun with Jen that I'd completely forgotten about work.

I pushed the glass door open and headed back to our table, my eyes resting on her as soon as I walked in.

Unfortunately, the warm excitement in my stomach wasn't the kind you're supposed to have on a family day out. It was more, and I could see through my fuzzy halo of intoxication that I was in trouble.

"Your boss?" she asked.

"Slash friend."

"I take it you're not going in tonight?"

I shook my head. "No. Not when you obviously need a babysitter."

"Shut up," she said, waving a hand in my direction. "I do not."

"Plus-" I scooted back in the booth, transfixed by the drunken sparkle in her eye. "Now that you're drunk, I was thinking I might stand a chance of scoring another kiss."

She froze, her eyes unblinking, and she held my gaze for a split second too long before casting her eyes down.

I furrowed my brow. "What?"

"I wasn't going to mention that again."

"Should I not have?"

She lifted her eyes to meet mine and lowered her voice. "Is it wrong that we did that?"

"According to who?" I asked, sliding my half empty glass of green stomachache towards me.

"I suppose you have a point."

"Anyway," I said. "I was only offering because I know you want to try it again, and I don't want you to feel weird about it."

She rolled her shiny eyes.

"What?"

"Trust me," she said. "If I wanted to kiss you again, I would."

I raised my eyebrows. "Oh, well that's a relief. I was worried you might still be totally repressed-"

"Excuse me?"

"And I'd hate for you to make out with your own hand when my perfectly capable lips are available."

She shook her head. "First of all, I haven't made out with my hand since I was fourteen."

"If you say so."

"And who says I even want to kiss you again?"

I leaned forward and fixed my eyes on her. "You're right."

"Thank you."

"You probably don't."

She folded her arms. "Yeah."

"But only because you're afraid you won't be able to stop there."

Her mouth fell open.

"Admit that you've had wet dreams about me."

"Girls don't have wet dreams."

I squinted at her. "Truth or dare?"

She swallowed and let her eyes drop to my lips before raising them again. "Truth."

I smiled. "Have you ever had an inappropriate thought about me? About us?"

She craned her neck back. "Define inappropriate."

"That's a fucking yes ladies and gentlemen."

"Don't be gross."

"Me?" I covered my chest with my hands. "You're the one having filthy thoughts about your stepbrother."

Her eyes darted around the packed bar. "Are you done?"

"Yeah. I'm done." And I was. After all, I wasn't about to take advantage of her when she was drunk, especially after the shit day she had.

But I needed to let her know that the thought of kissing her again had crossed my mind, and what better way to do that than by calling her out for having the same idea?

Besides, I was growing increasing less concerned about the consequences of wanting her. And I knew myself well enough to know that if things continued in this vein, I wasn't going to be able to keep my hands to myself.

"Truth or dare?" she asked.

I looked at her over my glass while I poured some more sweet tequila down my throat. "Truth."

"Do you want to be buried or cremated?"

I raised my eyebrows. "What the fuck? You're plotting my death now? I didn't mean to get you that wound up."

"No. I'm not plotting your death, and I'm not wound up by your childish teasing. I'm just curious."

I shrugged. "Well, I suppose I hate the idea of staying put for eternity, so cremated."

"And where do you want your ashes scattered?"

I yanked on the strings of my hoodie. "Can I change my answer if I think of something better?"

"Sure. Whatever."

"In that case, you know how they die the Chicago River Green on Paddy's Day?"

"Yeah."

"I'd liked to be dumped in there. On the actual day. Right in the middle of the goddamn party."

She stuck her lower lip out and nodded.

"What about you?"

"Can I change my answer if I think of something better?"

"Of course."

She cocked her head and one of her tank top straps fell off her shoulder.

I watched her slide it back up with her delicate fingers.

"Cremated for sure," she said.

"And where do you want your fairy dust sprinkled?"

"Maybe along the Golden Gate Bridge."

I furrowed my brow. "Why?"

"Cause then I'm bound to be in the movies eventually."

I rolled my eyes. "Yeah, but it'll be some Marvel flick or one of those new Planet of the Apes movies."

She shrugged. "That's okay. It's not like I'd get nominated for an Oscar playing ashes in the breeze anyway."

I leaned back and looked at her. I loved her ambition, loved how much she wanted to pursue her passion. I'd even go so far as to say she inspired me, making me wonder if it was time to pursue my own.

"Your turn to ask a question," she said lifting her chin.

I licked my salty lips. "What was your dare gonna be?"

She smiled. "Wouldn't you like to know?"

FLASHBACK
- Ethan -

I remember it like it was yesterday.

Aaron Schwartz was talking about dick sucking lips in the locker room. I always had a suspicion that he didn't have a mom based on the distasteful way he talked about women. I found out later it was true.

Anyway, I had just set my lacrosse gear down on the bench between us so I could undress and hit the showers.

"You know who has killer DSL that I'd love to try on?" he asked no one in particular.

A few guys murmured, egging him on. Not surprisingly, it was mostly the guys who were the least likely to find themselves with a pair of lips around their dick anytime soon.

"Jenny Layne."

I felt the hair on my neck stand up.

"You don't mind me saying that, do you Fitz?" he asked. "I mean, it's not like she's really your sister."

I raised my eyebrows and threw my shirt in the bottom of my locker. "Actually, I do mind."

"I thought you'd be more offended by what a nerd she is," he continued. "I mean, why does she hide that banging body under those thick sweaters, anyway?"

I raised a finger at him. "Leave it alone, Schwartz."

He ignored me and put one of his shoes up on the bench to untie it. "I was fucking wanking to the thought of her last night, and as soon as I imagined pulling that high ponytail up and down my dick, I busted a nut so big it was hard to imagine her being able to swall-"

I pushed him back against the lockers, the force of the impact causing the whole row to shake. "Don't fucking talk about her like that," I said. "She's too good for your sick fantasies."

"Whoa, whoa." He raised his palms between us. "How do you know she wouldn't like sucking my dick? You should let her decide for herself-"

I punched the locker next to his face.

"See what she says when I ask her to Homecomin-"

I laid my forearm against his throat and used the weight of my body to choke him hard against the lockers. "If you so much as look at her, I'll cut your fucking balls off and empty them down your own goddamn throat."

Apparently, some of the guys were telling me to lay off right about then, yelling at me about how Aaron was changing colors and shit.

But I didn't hear them. I couldn't hear anything over my anger, and hearing him degrade her like that- hearing him talk about her perfect pink lips- made me fucking snap in a way even I didn't see coming.

I kept my eyes on his until there was nothing left in them but fear. And when his hands finally dropped from my shoulders, I let him go.

He slumped to the ground gasping for air and burst into tears as soon as he caught his breath.

Then he called me all sorts of names.

But I didn't care.

Better me than Jenny.

He was too scared to tell the truth about what set me off when we got called down to the Dean's office, too. And I sure as hell wasn't going to repeat the garbage he'd spewed about her.

So it was my incomplete word against his.

I still maintain that he got what he deserved.

And I think the Dean was inclined to believe me.

Unfortunately, the black bruise across his skinny pale throat was enough to get me expelled.

It was probably the best and worst thing that ever happened to me.

Besides her, of course.

TWENTY THREE
- Jenny -

I woke up to the smell of a man.

It was the sweet smell of sweat mixed with something musky, something that made me think of the kind of rippling abs I associated with black and white cologne commercials.

Except I wasn't dreaming.

My eyes popped open.

I didn't know where I was.

Where was I supposed to be?

New York. A couch... Oh my god I was in Ethan's bed.

I lifted my head slowly and turned it the other way, establishing that I was, in fact, alone in Ethan's bed.

Had something happened?

I twisted around to look at the door. It was cracked open. I could hear him in the kitchen.

Fuck.

I sat up too fast, my brain sloshing inside my skull so hard I was afraid I might have internal bruising.

Why was I hungover in Ethan's bed?

Oh right. The incident. The tears. The bottomless margaritas.

I scooted up against the pillows and pulled the comforter up around me. I was in my underwear. My pajamas were thrown across the end of the bed. Neatly.

I rubbed my eyes, trying to remember what happened. I could recall leaving the restaurant, the shock of the cool evening air as it hit my face.

And then nothing.

What was it about the walk home that made it so hard to remember? I assumed that was an affliction that wouldn't stay with me after college.

But here I was again, clueless as fuck. Did he drive us? Surely not. He was shitfaced, too. Right?

So we must've walked. Or taken a cab?

Ugh. I hated the idea that I was walking around New York so out of it. Thank god I was with him.

Or so I was inclined to think. Shit. Normally, I didn't give a rats about the way home being fuzzy, but I minded this time.

Had I made an ass of myself?

Or kissed him again?

Not that I was put off by the idea, but not remembering wouldn't be okay.

I looked around his room, taking a moment to appreciate the view from the bed.

There was a closet to my left with mirrored, folding doors. A few strings of Mardi Gras beads hung off one of the door handles. A massive flat screen hung on the opposite wall, nearly blending in with the dark blue color scheme.

I leaned forward and stretched my fingers until they made contact with my pajamas. Then I slid them towards me and pulled my top on first before wriggling into my bottoms while I tried not to think about my bare ass tossing in his sheets all night.

I kept my eyes on the door and lifted one of his pillows up to my nose.

It smelled so good.

Was that just cologne or was it pheromones? Because if it was the latter then it wasn't my fault I was attracted to him. It was out of my control. I wondered what I smelled like to him, what it would be like to have him drop his face to my neck and breathe me in.

Perhaps there was still some alcohol in my system.

I set my feet on the floor and walked into the bathroom, flicking the light on as I raised my face to the mirror. My skin looked thirsty. I smeared some lotion under my eyes- just enough to give my skin a drink and wipe yesterday's mascara smudges away.

Then I used some of Ethan's mouthwash because brushing my teeth seemed too vigorous an activity for someone in my condition.

He didn't see me right away when I opened the door. He was buttering toast- with no shirt on. Had I touched his chest last night? To not remember that would be an even greater sin than if I had.

I leaned against the door frame, letting the smell of coffee wash over me like the irresistible paws of a thousand kittens.

"Morning, princess," Ethan said, lifting his eyes for a moment. "How did you sleep?"

"I'm not sure sleep is the word for what I was doing."

He lifted his chin towards the set table. "Help yourself to some painkillers."

"Just the breakfast I was hoping for," I said, taking a few steps to the closest chair.

He'd already put out two glasses of orange juice on ice. The one across from me was half drunk.

Kinda like myself.

I threw a few painkillers in my mouth and washed them down before taking a seat.

"Tequila, eh?" he said, the corner of his mouth clearly amused at my condition.

I pulled one knee up in front of me. "Bottomless margaritas seemed like such a good idea yesterday."

"That's how they get you," he said. "The problem is that it wasn't great tequila."

"How can you tell?"

"Because when it's great tequila, you wake up speaking Spanish with a mustache and no hangover to speak of."

I laughed. "I'll take a regular hangover, thanks."

"I'm surprised to hear you say that," he said, whipping some crème in a bowl, his muscular arm cocked and flexed beside him.

I scrunched my face. "Why?"

"Cause being able to grow a nice thick mustache would probably really increase the roles you could go up for."

"Perhaps. But only in shows I'm not trying to be in."

He laughed and spooned a dollop of crème on top of each of the tall coffee glasses in front of him.

"Those are fancy," I said.

"They're Irish."

"Does that mean there's whiskey in 'em?"

"Just a drop," he said. "To take the edge of."

"You're the expert."

He nodded. "And don't you forget it."

"So you feel like crap, too?"

He walked around the counter with a coffee in each hand. "Would it make you feel better if I said yes?"

"A little."

"I've felt better, yeah," he said, returning for the matching plates of eggs and toast.

"Thanks for doing this," I said, nodding towards the delicious looking spread.

He pulled his chair out and sat down. "Don't mention it."

"And with your special eggs and everything."

He smiled.

I picked up a fork. "What is it about being hungover that makes a buttery breakfast look so divine?"

"It's a mystery."

I stabbed some eggs and tried not to admire the way his Adam's apple moved as he swallowed his first bite of toast. "Speaking of mysteries…"

"Yeah?"

"Did you drive home last night?"

He raised his eyebrows. "You don't remember?"

I shook my head.

"We walked halfway and then got a cab."

"Right."

"The car's in a twenty four hour garage. I'll have to go pick it up this afternoon."

"I see." I tore a corner off my toast.

"Anything else you want to know?"

I raised my eyes to look at him.

He took a sip of his Irish coffee and licked some crème off his top lip.

I felt an ache in my guts.

It was the only ache in my body that actually felt good.

TWENTY FOUR
- Ethan -

She had that sexy bedhead thing going on like crazy.

If only she felt as good as she looked.

"Well?" I asked.

She raised her eyebrows. "Well what?"

"You want to ask me whatever question is obviously burning the tip of your tongue?"

She swallowed. "When you got up this morning-"

I squinted at her.

"Where exactly did you get up from?"

I smiled. "The couch. I got up from the couch."

She pursed her lips.

"Disappointed?" I took a sip of my Irish coffee.

"So nothing happened?"

"Oh, something happened all right."

Her lips fell apart.

"I decided after the day you had that you deserved to get a good night's sleep."

She tore a piece of her toast off with her teeth.

"And frankly, I really should've let you take the bed from day one so I apologize for that. From now on, I'll take the couch."

Her eyes grew wide. "You don't need to-"

"I do, actually."

"Well, you won't be inconvenienced for long."

I raised my eyebrows.

"Because as soon as I sober up, I'll have to head home and-"

I craned my neck forward. "Wait- what?"

"I only came for that audition and I blew it-"

"Please stop using that string of words to describe what happened."

"Sorry. I didn't get the part. Whatever," she said. "At least if I go home, I know Brandi's mom will give me a job at the salon, and as soon as I have enough money to come back and really make a go of it-"

I shook my head. "I can't believe I'm hearing this. Are you serious?"

"What other choice do I have?"

"Stay here and make another opportunity for yourself."

She sighed.

"What happened to no Plan B?"

"I'm not abandoning the plan," she said. "I'm doing what I have to do to make it work."

"I don't get why the hell you would leave when you came all the way here-"

"Because I can't just show up with an empty wallet and start sleeping in your bed. I'm, like, the biggest imposition ever."

"You're not." I leaned back. "I want you here."

She furrowed her brow. "What?"

"I've never done shit for you," I said. "Giving you a place to stay while you pursue your dream is the least I can do."

She narrowed her eyes at me.

"Really. It's my pleasure."

"But I'm totally cramping your style and-"

"In a good way."

One corner of her mouth curled up. "I don't even have a lead."

"You're a lot closer to your next lead if you stay here than you are if you go back and start spending the day spray tanning the local bridge club."

She bit her bottom lip.

"Honestly, I wouldn't offer if it wasn't okay."

She leaned back in her chair and drank some of her Irish coffee. "I tell you what, I could get used to those."

"They're easy to make. I can teach you."

She scrunched her face. "I bet they taste better when someone else makes them."

I rolled my eyes. "Fine. Whatever."

"Why do you care so much?" she asked, stabbing a clump of eggs with her fork.

There was no way I could tell her the truth. Where would I even start?

Because I've always cared? Because you make everything I like about this world seem within reach? Because making you laugh just once is enough to keep me smiling for a week straight?

Cause you're the hottest chick I know, and just knowing you're using my body wash gets me off even more than fucking other women?

She raised her eyebrows. "Well?"

"Cause if you leave now, that asshole wins."

Her eyes turned down at the corners.

"You can't give up just because you got a no."

"You mean just because I got assaulted."

I flinched at the thought of that creep looking at her mouth. "Fuck that guy, Jen. You're not here for him. You're here for you. And you haven't even been given a real chance yet." I sighed. "I just don't want you to leave before you get one."

She pulled another knee up and hugged them both to her chest.

"There's a thousand people getting a shot in this city every day, and one of those shots has your name on it."

"You think so?"

I nodded. "I know so."

"You're not so bad," she said, scooping some crème off the top of her coffee and sucking it off her finger.

I felt a twitch in my groin. "Sorry to disappoint."

She shook her head. "You've never disappointed me."

"Thanks."

"And I like thinking I could never disappoint you."

"You won't." I raised a finger towards her. "Unless you give up and go home."

She dropped her head and rested her chin on her knee.

"What do you say?" I asked. "You gonna give Plan A another shot?"

"I'm going to think about it."

"What's there to think about?" I asked, stacking her empty plate on mine.

"Money for one-"

"What do you need money for?"

She craned her neck forward. "To live? To eat?"

I furrowed my brow. "You think I'd let you go hungry?"

"No but-"

"I have plenty of money to feed us both, I assure you."

She pursed her lips.

"Even if you need to eat the occasional designer handbag."

She smiled.

I picked up the plates and walked over to the sink. "Besides," I said, turning on the tap. "You'd do it for me."

She laughed. "What? If you were a starving artist and showed up on my doorstep?"

"There are no starving artists here," I said. "And you've got to stop thinking of yourself that way if you're going to impress anyone in this city."

"What do you mean?"

I wiped our plates down with a soapy sponge. "I mean this city is full of bullshitters."

"What city isn't?"

"No, I mean bullshit is like a currency here. And the cost of living is high."

She squinted at me. "So I have to spend my bullshit like it's burning a hole in my pocket?"

"Let me put it another way," I said, rinsing the plates. "Have you ever heard that saying you have to fake it till you make it?"

"Of course."

"Well, that's what you have to do," I said. "The people you're trying to impress want confidence and magnetism. Stage presence."

"I know that."

"It's not enough to know it. You have to carry yourself like you're on a red carpet all the time."

She cocked her head.

"So you ooze star quality instead of vulnerability."

"I don't want to come across as a diva."

I pulled a dishtowel from under the sink. "You don't have to be a diva. You just have to keep your chin up."

"Uh-huh."

"So everyone you come across can tell you're the next best thing."

"Right."

"Then they won't be asking themselves if you're right for the part. They'll be thinking- can I afford to miss my chance at giving this future star her lucky break?"

"Mmm. I don't know."

"Trust me," I said, drying the plates. "I know what I'm talking about. Half my job is about live performance."

"Is that so?"

I stacked the dry plates next to the sink. "The only reason I have the sickest job in New York is because I bluffed my way to the top."

"I'm listening."

I leaned on the counter and looked at her. "I got my first job with a bullshit resume and a twinkle in my eye."

She rolled her eyes.

"I'd never made a drink for anyone but myself, and I'd only submitted my application for a bartending license two hours earlier."

"I get what you're saying, but maybe you're luckier than I am. Or more charming."

I shook my head. "No. The only difference is that I didn't think I had a Plan B."

"Plan A or bust then? That's your advice?"

I shrugged. "You got a better idea?"

TWENTY FIVE
- Jenny -

I knew Ethan was right.

I couldn't give up just because one horny asshole tried to get in my pants, or rather, tried to get me interested in his.

If anything, someday it would be nothing more than a story to put in the name and shame section of my tell all book.

But as far as today was concerned, I had work to do.

I set myself up on the couch and got ready to hunker down. If there was any truth to what Ethan had said, there were loads of casting calls going on that I could check out, maybe even today.

Or perhaps tomorrow as I was still a little hungover.

Regardless, I figured doing some research would help take the edge off- maybe not quite as well as that Irish coffee had- but still. And those eggs… How were they so much better than mine?

I mean, I realize he'd been living on his own for a while now, but they were way better. Maybe he used more butter. After all, more butter was always the answer.

Anyway, I wanted to have good news for him when he got back from collecting the car or going to the gym or whatever the heck he mumbled on the way out.

If he was going to be supportive and let me stay a bit longer, I didn't want him to think I was a completely useless slouch.

Besides, I didn't need my former professors to make my luck. I could do it myself. Heck, for all I knew, that shit yesterday happened for a reason, and I was never supposed to be Marilyn.

The perfect role might be waiting around the corner for me.

All I needed to do now was decide whether I could do better research if I nursed a small whiskey on the side.

Then again, if impressing Ethan was one of my goals, sticking with water was probably the way to go.

My phone rang as I opened my laptop, and I prayed it wasn't my mom calling to hear about yesterday.

For once, my prayers were answered.

"Hey."

"God, you could sound happier to hear from me," Brandi said. "Is it my Midwest accent that's grating on you now that everyone's calling you dahling?"

"I wish."

"You okay?"

"Yeah."

"Really?" she asked. "Cause you don't sound okay, and you blew off my calls like a mean girl yesterday."

"Sorry." I leaned back on the couch. "I'm just hungover."

"From drinking with Amy Schumer?"

"No. From drinking with Ethan."

"Even better!"

I winced. Her squealy tone was a bit more than I could take in my delicate state.

"Did you go out to celebrate your big break?"

I sighed. "Not exactly."

"If you're telling me some idiot failed to recognize your obvious talent then I'm going to have to come out there and kick some ass."

"Stay put. Ethan already offered."

"What happened?"

I bounced my crossed leg. "It wasn't that the director failed to recognize my talents."

"Go on."

"It was that he was interested in talents I wasn't willing to demonstrate."

"Like what?"

"Like giving blowjobs."

She gasped.

I waited for her to play my words over in her head.

"Wait, so he-"

"Yeah."

"And you-"

"Got the fuck out of there faster than you can say Hail Mary."

"Jesus."

"I know. How fucked up is that? I was so pathetically keen to impress him, too, ya know?"

"Did he just ask, like, point blank would you mind-"

"He got in my face and unzipped his zipper."

"Eww!"

"And said if I did him a favor, he'd do me one."

"I don't know what to say."

"Yeah. I didn't either. Which is just as well because it meant I wasn't at risk of opening my mouth and giving him the wrong idea."

"So you're okay?"

I shrugged. "Yes and no. But it's not like I'm the only woman that got sexually harassed in New York City yesterday."

"True, but that sounds like the kind of lottery I wouldn't be in a hurry to win again."

"No shit."

"I'm so sorry, Jen. That's hideous."

"Not as hideous as it would've been if I'd sucked his weasel dick."

"Obviously." She exhaled into the phone so hard it sounded like she was holding it out the window of a moving car. "So now what?"

"Now I'm going to see if I can find another audition to go to."

"Maybe bring mace next time."

"Not a bad idea."

"How long are you going to stay out there?" she asked. "I mean, I know you were planning on getting discovered and never coming home anyway-"

"That's not true."

"Oh please. You were too big for this town by sophomore year."

"Everyone is too big for our town."

"Are you going to keep staying with Ethan?"

"To be honest, I didn't want to impose, but he seems cool with it. Supportive even."

"Maybe he's grown up."

"He's definitely beefed up."

"Don't torture me."

I smiled.

"Has he tried anything?"

I furrowed my brow. "What do you mean?"

"Don't be stupid."

"I really don't know what you're talking about."

"I'm talking about the crush he's always had on you."

"He never had a crush on me."

"Oh please. No teenage boy is that mean to a teenage girl unless he's too sprung to know what's good for him."

"Or unless he's a bully."

"Which Ethan isn't. Except to you."

"That was a long time ago."

"It's not a theory, Jen. It's true whether you want to acknowledge it or not."

"So what?" I thought of the kiss, thought of how long he held me and made my lips feel like the center of the world. "Even if it were true, it's not like he would do anything about it. Not like he could."

"Why? Cause of all the respect he has for your parents? Yeah right. I think he definitely could."

I swallowed.

"And I think he would too if-"

"If what?"

"If he thought you were up for it."

"Which I'm not."

"Hey. Lie to yourself all you want, but don't fucking lie to me. You liked him before your parents got together and that never went away."

"Says you."

"Whatever. All I'm saying is that I think if all you do out there is investigate your career options, you're missing a trick."

"I'm not sure what you're getting at."

"Look. Don't get me wrong. If Ethan ever looked at me the way he looks at you even once, I already would've thrown myself at him so hard I would've stuck, but he never did. And he's a cool guy and insanely hot-"

"And my stepbrother, remember?"

"So what?"

I squeezed my eyes shut. "What do you mean so what?"

"I mean, I get why that stopped you before so many times. But you're not trapped in this nosy little town anymore. You graduated, and you're probably never going to live with your parents again."

"Fingers crossed."

"But you're always going to wonder about him," she said. "You're always going to wonder if the one that got away is the same one that's been within arm's reach this whole time."

I sighed.

"And if you aren't ready to admit that out loud, that's okay. But you need to realize that this is your chance to finally find out if there's something there."

"Why didn't you say any of this before?"

"Because," she said. "What good would it have done? You were thousands of miles apart and still living in fear of your folks. But you're not now. And even if it's just for five minutes, aren't you curious to know if that intense anger he has towards you is really just mutated passion?"

"And what if it is?" I asked. "What if you're right and he's crazy about me and doesn't give a shit what anyone has to say about it?"

"Then I'll envy you even more than I already do."

TWENTY SIX
- Ethan -

She was falling all over me last night.

Not that I minded.

On the contrary, she was so jubilantly drunk that I had half a mind to spill my guts, especially when she started repeating herself so much that I knew she wouldn't even remember.

Just the idea of confessing that I'd never had a sisterly thought about her in my whole life made me feel relieved. I couldn't imagine how freeing it would be to get the secret off my chest.

Unless, of course, it made her uncomfortable. Because that was the last thing I wanted. I'd rather take my feelings to the grave then upset her.

In fact, the thought of her being upset made me so unhappy I can only assume it was the reason I ended up drumming my fingers on the steering wheel outside Apple Seed Studios, trying to decide if I was going to pay the criminal casting director a visit.

So far, all I'd seen were young dancers and actors going in and out of the building. Or at least I had to assume that's what they were because I'd never seen so many people in leg warmers reading stapled pages while walking in all my life.

I took a deep breath, glanced at the clock, and leaned back in my seat.

Jen was so much prettier than the girls disappearing into the building ahead. She had a timeless grace about her that I never tired of.

She could hold your attention like a flower in a gentle breeze. Delicate, but strong. God I was so proud of her for telling that guy where to stick it yesterday.

When we were walking home last night, she bent over in the middle of the sidewalk and took her shoes off. I suppose that's when I knew she was a few margaritas past memory recall.

And as soon as we got in the cab, she curled up into a ball and laid down in my lap. I pulled her hair out of her face with my fingertips and dragged them gently across her temple.

I couldn't help it.

It would be like holding one of my favorite paintings from the MoMA in my lap and not touching it.

When we got back to my building, I carried her from the elevator to the door, setting her down against the wall so I could make sure she didn't stumble as I let us in.

And as soon as she stepped inside, she turned, put her hands against my chest, and leaned into me.

I held her against me, kissed her forehead, and inhaled. Her hair smelled like candy apples.

She didn't put up a fuss when I grabbed her pajamas and brought her to my room.

Then I closed the door and lied awake on the couch for hours, wondering how the hell I was going to tell her that being around her was torturous for me and that I desperately wanted her to stay.

Somehow I'd managed that last part this morning.

But when she asked if anything happened, I didn't tell her the whole truth.

Because if I had, she would already know that I'd fallen for every sexy, brave inch of her, and that I didn't give a fuck what anyone else had to say about it.

Least of all my dad.

After all, he'd had two loves in his life.

Just like me.

Except I'd always believed I had to keep my affections for both hidden... though I was starting to think the real source of my shame was the fact that I'd put off pursuing them both for so long.

I leaned forward, rested my forehead on the steering wheel, and clenched my jaw, knowing that if I got within two feet of the motherfucker who came onto her yesterday, there was a very good chance I wouldn't waste the trip.

Once my fist made contact with his face, I'd be off, just like I was in all those fights I got into on the playground after my mom died. Except I was a lot bigger now.

And while I was giddy at the thought that I could send that guy to the hospital with two wrists so broken he'd never touch a hair on another trusting young woman's head again, the longer I sat there, the more I realized that not only was I not that guy anymore, but that I didn't want to be.

Plus, what would it accomplish?

Sure, he'd get a fraction of what he deserved, but Jenny would probably be disappointed in me considering she knew how many fucking anger management courses I've been subjected to in the past.

What's more, it wouldn't help her get ahead. Nor me. I could jeopardize my job and my relationship with my friends, including my own boss. Worst of all, it might make Jenny uneasy, and she didn't deserve that.

Besides, she wasn't a nerdy kid anymore. My rage was no use to her.

What she needed was my support, which I'd tried to lend her this morning. And I thought I'd done a decent job, too, whereas punching this guy's lights out would probably be a step backwards.

I flipped my visor down to block the view of the studio's entrance and pulled out my phone.

Christophe answered on the third ring.

"I need some advice."

He laughed. "Legal or sexual?"

I rolled my eyes. "Legal."

"Shoot."

"How do you go after a sexual predator?"

"I need more information."

I sighed. "My stepsister got assaulted on a casting call yesterday. The guy basically whipped it out and asked her to open wide."

"Jesus. Even I'm smoother than that."

"I've heard mixed opinions."

"So what do you want to know? How to see justice done?"

"Pretty much."

"Can I assume you're calling because you've wisely decided not to take matters into your own hands?"

"You know me so well."

"Right. In that case, there are two options."

"Go on."

"We can get a bunch of testimonials from individuals who've suffered the same injustice."

"And if that's not an option?"

"You can file a complaint with the police," he said. "Which is useless, but it might help you sleep better at night."

"Uh-huh."

"Not the information you were looking for, I take it?"

I shrugged. "I thought you were more legit than that. I thought you'd have a plan to bug the guy's office and set a trap."

"I don't play a lawyer on TV, Ethan. I really am one."

"Mmm."

"Sorry to disappoint."

"So no full scale investigation?"

"Cause some asswipe looked at your sister funny?"

"Stepsister."

"Regardless, no can do."

I sighed.

"Though you should file a complaint with the police, if only to get the guy on their radar."

"Will do."

"Anything else I can help you with?"

I was about to say no when I had an idea. "Actually, there is."

"Shoot."

"You know how you were saying your uncle has a talent agency?"

"Yeah."

"Think you could send me the details?" I asked.

"Would you consider it a personal favor for which you'd owe me one?"

"Sure."

"No problem," he said. "Give me till the end of the day, and I'll give him a heads up."

"Thanks, clown."

"Anytime."

I turned the phone off, feeling even better than if I'd done what I went there to do.

Now I was just two more calls away from another epic afternoon.

TWENTY SEVEN
- Jenny -

I was checking the location of my leads on Google Maps when he called, and the flutter of warmth I felt in my chest when his name popped up on the screen made me want to doodle his name in pink pen.

"How's the head?" he asked.

"Pretty useless."

"You back in bed?"

My eyes grew wide. Did he really think I would just lounge around in his bed when he wasn't here?

How inappropriate would that be?!

More inappropriate than the fact that I'd smelled his pillow that morning?

"No." Or was I in his bed? Was the couch his bed now? "I've been scouring the internet to find out what other casting calls are going on and-"

"Any joy?"

I shrugged. "Some. It's hard to tell if I'm not familiar with the production. For example, one of the shows sounds really vague. I think I'd be auditioning for the role of some sort of spice?"

"Like frankincense and myrrh or more like baby and scary?"

"The former, actually. And I didn't realize you were a fan of the Spice Girls?"

"I'm not," he said. "I only know that because they came into the club last fall."

"Damn. Really?"

"Yeah. I could barely contain my excitement."

I smiled. "What did they drink?"

"Would you rather I make something up or admit that I don't remember?"

"Mmm. I suppose the truth is better."

"Always or-"

"Always," I said, feeling like a huge hypocrite.

"Well then- while we're on the topic of honesty- I have some good news."

"I could use some," I said. "Can I guess?" What was I twelve? Was I just that desperate to keep him on the phone?

"Sure."

"You've found a cure for hangovers?"

"I'm afraid the closest I've gotten is that drink I made you this morning."

I pursed my lips. "You won the lottery and you're dying to produce my first indie flick."

"You got a script?"

"No."

"I never produce without a script."

I sighed.

"You got us tickets to Wicked."

"Seriously?"

I scrunched my face.

"Do you really think that's what it is?"

"A girl can dream."

"You like musicals?"

"I like live theater of any kind."

"I bet you a million dollars that you don't."

I craned my neck back. "What kind of show wouldn't I like?"

"I don't even know where to start. Vagina Olympics in Bangkok, sex shows in Amsterdam-"

My face dropped.

"The cat circus in Moscow."

"That last one sounds okay."

"It's not. It's totally not okay."

My lips fell apart.

"Have you ever even met a cat?" he asked.

"Fine. I owe you a million dollars."

"I know," he said. "But I'll waive the fee on one condition."

"I'm listening."

"Have dinner with me."

"Dinner?"

"Yeah. I took tonight off work to spend time with you. Seems like the least I could do if you don't know how long you're sticking around."

I swallowed.

"Besides, I don't have any food in the fridge, which I'm sure you noticed. So what do you say?"

"Okay."

"Great."

I furrowed my brow. "Is that the good news? That we're going out to eat?"

"Not officially."

"What's officially the good news?"

"It's a two-parter."

I leaned forward to rest my elbows on my knees. "Go on."

"Part one is that I didn't go beat the shit out of that pervert that upset you yesterday."

"What?"

"I thought about it, and I was pretty close, but I decided committing murder on a sunny Friday morning wouldn't be as gratifying in real life as it was in my imagination."

"I'm glad you made the right decision."

"He's still on my shit list, though, so if you start having nightmares of something-"

"I'll let you know."

"Good."

"Is that it then? The good news is that you decided to be a mature adult for two seconds and not use violence to solve problems that aren't even yours."

"Actually, it gets better."

"Gee. I don't know if anything could be better than the fact that you're not calling from prison, but try me."

"I got you a lead."

"A lead?"

"More like a meeting. With a real agent."

"An agent?"

"Yeah. My buddy's uncle runs a place in Midtown, and he's agreed to meet with you.

"Wow."

"Not too shabby for a hungover half day's work."

"Not at all," I said. "That is good news."

"So I'll take you somewhere fancy, and we'll celebrate over steaks."

I cocked my head. "Will it be so fancy we won't be able to order biscuits as a starter?"

"Of course. Unless you're homesick, in which case I believe there's a Bob Evans in Buffalo."

"That's okay. I think I can last a while longer without."

"Great. Then I know just the place."

"This is all really nice of you, Ethan, but it's not helping me feel like I'm not imposing."

"That's your problem. Not mine."

"And I feel a bit awkward knowing you've been worrying about me since you left the apartment."

Silence.

"Not to call you out."

"That's exactly what you did."

I smiled. "You can make up for it by not thinking about me at all until dinner."

"Sounds easy enough. Deal."

"Text me the address, and I'll meet you there."

"I'd rather send a car and call you when it's outside."

"Okay."

I hung up the phone and set it down.

What if Brandi was right?

I thought about the kiss and the way he'd joked about it yesterday over drinks.

What if his heart wasn't in being just my stepbrother? What if it never had been?

Any idiot could see how amazing he was. He was funny, smart, and tough as he was sexy. Plus, he had a cool job in a cool place.

But why would he be into me?

I understood the attention when I was fourteen. I was weird. Other. I stuck out like a sore thumb. Or at least, that's why I always thought he stared.

But there were years then when he hardly spoke to me at all. Why would he have treated me like that for so long? Because he liked me when he shouldn't have?

Part of me wanted to believe Brandi was full of shit.

After all, it wouldn't be the first time. She was notorious for looking for drama where none existed, but I don't think she would do that with my life.

Sure, she might roast me royally behind closed doors, but she'd bent over backwards to keep me from looking stupid when we were growing up. If she had any doubt about Ethan's feelings, she wouldn't tease me or egg me on. That wasn't like her.

And what if this trip really was my last chance to figure out what we actually meant to each other?

I mean, if I let my guard down and he sensed it, there were only two things that could happen.

Either he'd get freaked out, in which case I'd laugh my flirtation off as a joke and let the weirdness dissipate over the following days.

Or, he'd take the chance I gave him with both hands, and I'd finally get to find out if the years of sexual frustration I'd endured were based on something deeper than simply wanting what I thought I couldn't have.

And, to be honest, the possibility of option two excited me so much I knew it was worth considering.

Now I just had to decide what to wear.

TWENTY EIGHT
- Ethan -

I tightened my hand around the yellow daisies and then loosened my grip.

I'd done it so many times I was surprised I hadn't torn the plastic cover around the stems.

"Would you like another-?" The bartender nodded at my drink.

"No, thanks," I said, looking down at my half full beer. Who did this clown think he was? It was way too early to start pushing drinks on people.

However, it was definitely not too early for Jenny to walk through the door.

I hoped she would like the place. It was classy and dark, but not too stuffy.

And it was the least I could do to take her somewhere half decent after drowning her in cheap margaritas and finger food last night.

I exhaled and put my elbows on the bar. What was it about her that made me so crazy?

On one hand, I'd love if she got that hammered again because she was so fun when she let her guard down, when she didn't read too much into it when I gave her a compliment.

On the other hand, it had taken every ounce of restraint I had last night not to kiss her again, not to run my hands over her hips and pull her close. And I knew well enough to know that I was no saint or superhero. It was unlikely that I could display that kind of control again, especially two nights in a row.

Then again, what if I did kiss her? What was the worst thing that could happen?

She might slap me. Or never speak to me again. It's not like that would be all that terrible.

After all, it would be better than if she never laid a hand on me, and it's not like we were fucking pen pals. If she stopped talking to me when she left the city, everything would be pretty much the same as it had always been.

If anything, it might be better to try something and risk driving her away. At least I might stand a chance of being able to move on then. But the more time I spent with her, the more far flung that idea seemed.

I looked towards the fire pit at the front of the restaurant just in time to see her walk in. She was wearing a little yellow dress and looked like she was rising up from the flames as she passed by the fire.

I felt my chest swell as she greeted the hostess, and a lump formed in my throat when they started towards me.

I stood up, feeling weak in the knees as I noticed her smooth legs sticking out from the bottom of her dress. Then I forced my eyes up to the wide scoop neckline where two thin straps hung over her collarbones.

I recalled the last time I saw her showing so much skin.

It was at a pool party shortly after our parents got married. She wasn't really invited to the party. She was just there because she was friends with my buddy's younger sister. They kept to themselves the whole time, laughing and passing magazines back and forth.

It drove me fucking crazy.

I wanted her to notice me, to watch me like I watched her.

Instead, she just laid there in her ruffled turquoise bikini, completely oblivious to me. And I swear I couldn't have been more impressed by a woman's beauty than if I were the Greek peasant who first laid eyes on the Venus de Milo.

"Hi," I said when she walked up.

"Your table is ready," the hostess said. "Right this way."

I gestured for Jenny to go first and stepped behind her, my thoughts obsessed by how the flirty bottom of her dress fluttered below her ass.

Boy was I in trouble.

I would've pulled Jen's chair out, but the hostess beat me to it, and as we took our seats, she remarked that we were a very handsome couple.

I swallowed and opened my mouth to speak, but Jenny just nodded and said thank you, smiling at the woman like we got that all the time as she accepted her menu.

"Are those for me?" Jenny asked, nodding towards the flowers in my hand after the hostess left.

I looked at them for a moment like I wasn't sure whose arm I was staring at before snapping out of it. "They are, yeah," I said, handing the daisies across the table.

"Thanks," she said, reaching for them. She closed her eyes as she brought them to her nose, her lashes long against her cheeks. "What's the occasion?"

I shrugged. "I just figured you might as well get used to getting flowers since it won't be long before it's happening every night of the week."

Her eyes sprang into little crescents. "Thanks," she said, laying them at the edge of the table. "I hope you're right."

I smiled.

"And I love that they match my dress."

"Which is stunning by the way."

She fixed her eyes on mine. "Stunning?"

"Yeah."

She swallowed.

I leaned back in my chair. "Unless it makes you uncomfortable for me to say that in which case-"

"What?" She squinted at me. "You take it back?"

I pursed my lips.

"It's fine," she said.

"Good. Cause I'd be lying if I took it back."

"And for the record-"

I raised my eyebrows.

"Your attention has never made me uncomfortable."

I narrowed my eyes at her.

"What makes me uncomfortable is-"

"What?"

"This thing that hangs over us that makes everything so weird all the time."

I clenched my jaw.

She opened her menu. "I just wish things were different."

I turned an ear towards her. "What do you mean?"

She shrugged. "I don't know."

I took a deep breath.

"I mean, I can't say I wish our parents never got married. Because they're happy together most of the time and-"

I furrowed my brow. "And what?"

"And I wouldn't begrudge them that." She looked down at her menu. "Especially after what they've both been through."

I looked at the daisies and then back at Jen, wondering what my mom would've thought of her. "Of course."

"But I never wanted you to be my stepbrother."

"But I'm so great at it."

She laughed.

The melodic sound made my chest loosen.

"You aren't great at it," she said. "You've never been anything but a pain in my ass."

"I'm sorry. I should've been a better-"

"You're not listening," she said. "I never wanted you to be a better stepbrother. I never even wanted a brother."

"What did you want?"

She kept her head tilted down but let her eyes flick up at me. "Wouldn't you like to know?"

"Yeah. I would."

"So." She smiled. "Tell me about the agency you mentioned on the phone."

Why couldn't she just admit that she always wanted me, too, and put me out of my misery?

Why did she have to be so gorgeous and enigmatic and out of reach?

Or was she trying to tell me she wasn't?

And that she never had been?

TWENTY NINE
- Jenny -

There was no question that he checked me out when I walked in.

Of course, I was hoping he would. I wouldn't have worn such a flirty dress otherwise.

But I thought he'd be more subtle about it. Instead, he checked me out like he couldn't even help himself, like he didn't give a shit who noticed.

No wonder the hostess thought we were a couple.

And as soon as I felt his eyes skim over my body like that I swear I felt flames shoot up my spine. It was the best feeling ever. I half expected my head to float away like a balloon after it happened.

But the sound of his voice made me feel grounded all over again.

I rarely showed so much skin. I mean, if there was anything I couldn't live without, it would be my collection of oversized sweaters.

But the thought of Ethan's eyes resting on parts of me that were usually covered excited me, and when I slipped the little dress on, it was almost like wearing a costume. And I'd always felt confident in costumes.

Besides, I was going to need that confidence tonight if I was going to break my own rules and fill my night with firsts.

As I was getting ready, I tried to remember the last time I exposed so much skin around him. It had been a rare occurrence.

After all, the few times he came home after he got sent away were all over Christmas breaks. He must've seen me in nothing but sweaters and leggings for years on end.

And then it came to me. It was one day at Kelsey's house when her brother was having a pool party. I still remember the turquoise bikini I was wearing at the time. It had ruffles.

Anyway, I was young enough that sexual energy was still a total mystery to me, but I remember being conscious of how I laid across the deck chair, as if I were channeling Elizabeth Taylor in Cleopatra or something.

What a joke. I'm not even sure if he noticed me that day. He was so busy playing chicken with the other popular kids, getting dunked by the older girls so frequently it made my blood boil.

"So obviously he couldn't promise me anything," Ethan said. "But at least the guy has some connections and said he'd be happy to try and help you any way that he can."

"Well, I can't thank you enough." I smoothed my napkin over my lap. "Even if he can't do anything for me, just the experience of getting in front of someone is a step in the right direction."

"Did you have any luck online today?" he asked, biting his piece of bruschetta in half.

I shrugged. "It's hard to say." I took a slice of bruschetta from the center of the table and set it on my bread plate. "I mean, there is clearly enough work out there that I could get something. However, a few of the gigs I found might not be a step in the right direction for my dignity, if that makes sense."

He laughed. "It does, and I hate to break it to you, but the fact that there's something for everyone in this city is both the best and worst thing about it."

"Trust me, after checking Craig's list today, I believe that more than ever."

"Just be careful," he said, his face suddenly serious.

I felt my chest tighten.

"If you even feel moderately sketchy about a job, either don't go, or ask me to come with you."

"Okay."

"Promise me, Jenny."

"I promise."

"Good. That should help me make progress on how pissed I still am about what happened to you yesterday."

I raised my eyebrows. "Are you still not over that? Even I'm over it. Sexual harassment happens, Ethan."

"Not to you it doesn't," he said. "Not on my watch."

I hated that he was still torn up about it, but I loved the fact that there was actually a man in my life who wanted to protect me. It felt good in a way that I wanted to believe I deserved.

And it reminded me of something my mom said once about Ethan's dad. She said, "I don't care that he's controlling, Jenny. I don't care that he's set in his ways and that his time in the army will always affect his personality. And I don't care if other people think the standards he holds people to are extreme. All I care about is that he would go to his grave trying to protect the things he loves, and I'm lucky to be one of those things."

And for a split second, it occurred to me that maybe Ethan and his dad weren't as different as Ethan wanted to believe.

"You enjoying that?" he asked.

I covered my chewing mouth, nodded, and swallowed. "More than I want to admit."

"Good."

"Don't judge me, but Brandi and I ordered bruschetta at a restaurant at home last summer-"

"Mistake."

"I know," I said. "But I always wanted to try it."

"I'm afraid for where this story is going."

"They were out of tomatoes."

He shook his head.

"So they used ketchup."

He raised his eyebrows. "So you essentially ate subpar pizza bread."

"It wasn't great."

He smiled. "There's a shock."

"Can I ask you something?"

"Shoot," he said, leaning back in his chair. His collared shirt gaped open at the top just enough to keep my eyes from straying too far.

"What is it that you love so much about bartending?" I asked, taking a sip of my white wine. "I mean, I know I've been rambling on about my acting so I'm just curious…"

"There's a lot I like about it," he said. "I like that I can always get better at it. I like that it's something other people appreciate, something that's going to be in demand for a long time to come."

"True."

"And I like that I work around people who are out to have a good time."

"Understandable."

"I guess after all that time in boarding school where everything was so regimented and where having too much fun was not only frowned upon but subject to disciplinary action, it's a relief to spend time in an environment that's refreshingly unpredictable."

"Mmm."

"For example." He fixed his eyes on me. "I don't know if you know this, but in Russia, little kids are taught in school that they shouldn't go around smiling because it comes across as needy and disingenuous. Same with people in the workforce. If you're engaged in serious business- whether you're in sales or waitressing or a postal worker- then you shouldn't be smiling."

I furrowed my brow. "What?"

"And you definitely aren't supposed to smile at strangers because they don't know you so it's considered weird behavior."

I shook my head. "I had no idea. That sounds so hostile."

He shrugged. "It's just a cultural quirk. And I haven't seen it myself, but my buddy goes to Russia for work a lot, and he basically has to get his smiling under control or risk not being taken seriously."

"That's insane."

"It's exhausting is what it is," he said. "And that's what boarding school was like for me. Year after year of smiling being treated as suspicious behavior."

"Whoa."

"Don't get me wrong. I needed to go. I had no respect for authority, and I was channeling my energy in all the wrong ways."

"Yeah."

"But now I just want to be around people who fucking want to smile and have a good time."

"That makes perfect sense."

"So for the record, I won't be looking for work in Moscow anytime soon," he said. "After all, I'd much rather be smiling here with you."

THIRTY
- Ethan -

"What's the damage?" she asked when the bill came.

"None of your business," I said, sliding my card in the small leather folder.

She furrowed her brow. "Are you sure? I really don't mind paying my way."

"Someday you can get me back when you're a big star."

She smiled. "I like the sound of that."

The evening air was warm and energizing when we hit the sidewalk, and I was already wishing it were earlier. I had so much more to say to her, and I just wasn't sure how I was going to do it.

"What would you like to do?" I asked. "Go for a drink? Try and get some scalped tickets for a show?"

"I think you've spent enough on me tonight," she said, her hand with the flowers swinging beside her. "Plus, last night was pretty boozy."

"You bounced back well enough."

"Yeah, but I'd be happy to just go back and have a glass of wine. Listen to some music. Is that totally lame on a Friday night?"

"Not at all," I said. "Lame is not doing what you want. And I'm always out on a Friday so I'm absolutely fine with that plan."

"Great," she said. "We'll pick something up on the walk home."

"No need," I said. "I've got more wine at my place than-"

"Condoms?"

I raised my eyebrows. "What?"

"Sorry," she said, her cheeks blushing. "I might have accidentally seen that you're hoarding condoms for the apocalypse."

I rolled my eyes. They never seemed to last very long, but I wasn't about to tell her that. "Did you go through all my drawers or just my underwear drawer?"

"Just that one," she said. "The day I arrived. But I swear I stopped snooping as soon as I saw your stash."

Half my mouth curled into a smile, and I nodded across the street. "Let's cut through the park."

"I shouldn't have mentioned it," she said, her hair shining under the street lights as we crossed in front of the stalled traffic. "Besides, I suppose it would be more embarrassing for you if you didn't have condoms at your place."

"That's right," I said, stepping to the side so she could walk through the black iron gates into the park. "Is there anything else you want to ask me since we're suddenly discussing my sex life?"

She stopped in her tracks.

I turned back to look at her, realizing I was far more amused than she was.

"Oh god." She scrunched her face. "We were having such a nice time and then I had to blow it by being awkward."

"Hey." I squared my shoulders to face her. "You're not awkward." I glanced down at her lips. "You're funny and charming, and I couldn't care less that you went through my shit."

She covered her face with her hands.

I grabbed her wrists and pulled them down so I could see her shiny eyes again. "Jenny."

She squinted. "What?"

"Pull it together so we can take this conversation about your fascination with my condom collection back to mine."

She swallowed.

"Hell, I'll even model a few of them for you if you want-"

She pushed my chest away. "Don't be stupid."

I grabbed her shoulders and pressed my cheek against hers so I could whisper in her ear. "Don't pretend the thought hasn't crossed your mind."

"It has." She spoke so softly her words were like a breeze. "Does that make me terrible?"

"No," I said, loosening the grip I had on her when I realized I was touching her bare flesh. "Not any more terrible than me anyway."

She craned her neck back and looked at me, her eyes searching mine. "Really?"

I dropped my hands. "I might be a prick, but I'm not a liar."

Her lips fell apart.

"Come on," I said, tilting my head behind me. "Let's get out of-"

"Wait," she said, laying her free hand on my chest and staring at it.

Her hand on my body made me feel hot all over.

She looked up at me, letting her eyes drop to my mouth.

And I went for it, pressing my lips against hers in the middle of the public park.

She leaned into me and slipped her tongue in my mouth.

I slid my hands around her lower back, pulling her against my hips as I swelled for her and sucked the sweetness from her wine soaked tongue.

It was a long kiss, and it might've been even longer if an eruption of applause hadn't interrupted us so soon.

Jenny pulled back and looked past me.

I looked over my shoulder and saw half a dozen teenage boys drinking poorly disguised cans of beer down the path to our left. When I looked back at Jenny, she was flushed.

The cheering continued.

"I wonder would they be clapping if they knew," she said.

"To be honest, I think they'd be clapping if I was a squirrel who just found a nut."

"Perhaps," she said, starting towards the path that led away from the boys.

"Though I suppose I feel much the same way."

"What do you mean?" she asked, hooking her arm around mine.

"I mean now that you're here, it feels like I've found something I misplaced."

She glanced at me.

"I don't know if that makes sense-"

"It does," she said. "Though I'm not sure misplaced is the right word."

I furrowed my brow. "What would be the right word?"

"Misunderstood?"

"Mmm." I walked along beside her, my chest bursting like fireworks as I tried to make sense of what just happened.

"Ethan?"

"Yeah?"

"What are we going to do now?"

"We're going to go back to my apartment like we discussed."

"Uh-huh."

"And then we're going to have a few glasses of wine and listen to some music."

"Okay."

"And then we're going to do whatever we want because that's the theme of the night."

She swallowed.

"And we won't overthink anything until tomorrow morning."

"I like that idea."

I turned towards her. Her face was glowing from the kissing and the wine, and I swear she'd never looked more beautiful. "Yeah?"

She nodded. "That sounds like the kind of fun I've wanted to have for a long time."

I smiled. "You and me both, Jenny. You and me both."

THIRTY ONE
- Jenny -

I couldn't believe he kissed me in public.

No one had ever done that.

And he was probably the last person who ever should've.

And yet, I wasn't sorry. Not even a little bit. On the contrary, I felt full where I usually felt empty, warm where I usually felt cold, light where I usually felt heavy.

So it couldn't be wrong, could it?

Then again, my heart wasn't exactly the most insightful moral compass. Even on a good day, it was completely untrustworthy.

But even if I didn't feel I could trust myself, surely I could trust Ethan.

He clearly wanted what was best for me- his kisses being at the top of the list.

We were quiet on the way home.

Sure, it was that kind of quiet where you get the sense that both people are walking along having really loud thoughts, but none of them were spoken out loud... not since we both agreed that an evening of music and wine and not overthinking things was just what we needed.

Of course, that was a lot easier said than done.

I mean, I was totally overthinking things- namely his lighthearted joke about modeling condoms for me, which I found both exciting and terrifying. But it was that magnetic kind of fear that makes people go to scary movies and set foot in haunted houses.

In other words, I was pretty sure my desire to be vulnerable with him was starting to outweigh my fear of the awkward aftermath that might result.

Needless to say, I was relieved when he opened the wine as soon as we walked in the door.

I slipped my shoes off while he poured two glasses of white.

Then he disappeared to his room for a second, returning a few moments later as some music began to play.

"So," I said, taking a sip. "What's new?"

He laughed. "Besides kissing you?"

I dug my toes into the light carpet and searched his eyes. "It was better this time, wasn't it?"

"Yeah," he said. "Cause we were us. Instead of Marilyn and Brian."

I smiled. "We're better as us."

He nodded. "I think so."

"Wanna dance?"

He scrunched his face.

"Don't pretend you've never danced to Bowie in your apartment."

"How about you dance and I watch," he said, taking a sip of his drink.

"How about you touch me when I ask you to?"

His eyes grew wide.

"I don't bite, you know."

"That's not what I'm afraid of."

I drained half my glass and set it down on the counter. "What are you afraid of?"

He sighed.

I stepped into his personal space and looked up at him. The electricity between us was thick and warm. "Tell me."

He scooted his glass down and looked at me, his eyes sweeping over my face and my chest with zero subtlety. "I'm afraid I won't be able to stop if I start."

"What? Dancing?"

"No." He trailed his fingertips up the side of my arm. "Touching you."

My chest tightened around my racing heart.

His eyes were dark and full of lust.

"Don't be," I said, laying a hand on his jaw. "I promise I won't ask you to."

He kissed me again a second later, pulling me against him with a force much greater than he'd used in the park.

I swirled my tongue around his and felt his hands curl underneath my dress, his flat palms sliding over my body a second later.

I pulled away from him just long enough for him to pull my dress off over my head.

"Fuck, Jenny," he said, his large hands undoing the clasp on my strapless bra. "You don't know how much I've wanted this." He planted his lips against mine again and slid his hands over my breasts.

My nipples hardened against his palms and a coil of heat curled in my stomach.

I clasped my hands behind his neck and leaned my hips against him, letting his tongue erase my mind.

A second later, his hands were under my ass, lifting me up.

I wrapped my legs around his waist and held on as he carried me over to the couch.

When he sat down, his lips strayed from mine and traveled down my neck, effectively loosening it so it fell to the side, his lips burning their way down my collarbone to my breasts.

He groaned as he sucked one of my nipples into his mouth, flicking it with his tongue as he kneaded my other breast in his large hand.

I could feel his dick swelling between my legs, the hard length of it along my slit.

And in that moment he wasn't the only one who was afraid. I was afraid, too- of how much I wanted him, of how much I was willing to give him, of how much I didn't care that he was going to take it without asking.

And I knew that I would keep my promise, that I wouldn't stop him.

I rocked against his dick, growing wetter with his every squeeze and swell.

"Ethan," I whispered as he sucked my breasts.

He threw me down on the couch and knelt over me, unbuttoning his shirt without taking his eyes off mine.

I watched as he showed me his abs again. But for the first time, I didn't try to look away.

Then his hands were on his belt, pulling it from the loops. The sound of his zipper going down made every hair on my body stand up.

But he kept his boxers on.

Then he wrapped his fingers around the sides of my small white panties and slid them down, his eyes devouring every inch of me as he did it.

I stared at the outline of his cock where it was straining against his grey boxers and felt a rush unlike anything I'd ever known.

And when he lowered his head between my knees, I knew a line had been crossed.

Nothing would ever be the same.

I raised my hands over my head as he laid his tongue against me, gushing against him as he flicked my swollen bud.

And when he started moving his tongue faster, I pulled my own hair and arched my back, spilling into his mouth with a groan.

The pleasure was unbearable, and I felt like a ray of light, bending with his will.

"Oh god, Ethan," I whispered, his name on my lips like a bad word as my hips bucked against his face. "That feels so good."

He pinned me down with his free hand, spreading it across my stomach while the other fucked me deep and hard, his fingers curling against my core.

I was burning up, and I felt all the heat inside me pool between my legs. "I'm gonna come," I mouthed, but no sound escaped.

And when my body jerked one last time, he pulled his fingers from inside me and drank my pleasure down like he'd been waiting his whole life to taste me, his lips slurping against my wet hot center.

And in that moment, I didn't have a single regret.

I mean, how could I?

I was pure stardust.

THIRTY TWO
- Ethan -

I was convinced I was dreaming, but I didn't dare pinch myself.

She was even more vivacious than I ever imagined.

Not only did she taste as light as strawberry water, but her body was fucking perfect. Every curve I came across was more gorgeous than the last, and I couldn't get enough of the way she responded to my touch.

I kissed her pussy one last time and wiped my lips on the delicate flesh of her inner thigh before kissing my way up her soft stomach and her panting chest.

When I was suspended over her, she looked at me through half closed eyes.

She smiled. "That's by far the nicest thing you've ever done for me."

I laughed. "I'm not sure if that's a compliment considering there's not much competition."

"Oh, it is."

I stared back and forth between her hazel eyes, admiring the way the flush of her cheeks framed her light freckles. "You taste like heaven."

She pursed her lips. "And you feel like it."

"You haven't felt anything yet," I said, pressing my hard on against her throbbing heat.

She reached up and pulled my face down to hers, opening her mouth wide to kiss me. "Hurry up," she whispered against my lips. "Before I change my mind."

I straightened up and pulled my boxers down.

Having her eyes on my cock was almost enough to make me bust my load right there. And I might've, too. God knows how many times I imagined what she would look like covered in me. But those were the dark fantasies I had for her.

And those thoughts had no place here, not when she was so naked and vulnerable and full of obvious trust in me.

I wouldn't degrade her like that… unless she asked me to.

But it was too soon for that.

This was too new.

Besides, what I wanted most was to know what it felt like to be inside her. Deep. Like she'd always been in me.

I bent over and scooped her up, setting her feet down on the couch so she was standing on it, my head level with her breasts.

She looked down at me and dragged her fingertips against the sides of my head.

I slid my hand back between her legs and let her sweet nectar drip on my fingers.

"I want you inside me," she whispered. "Please."

I pulled her arms around my neck and lifted her off the couch. I wanted her in my bed. I wanted her hair against my pillows and her smell between my sheets.

But when I got to the door, I didn't walk through it. Instead, I pressed her back up against the wall and reached for my dick.

Then I pressed the tip of it against her opening and let her slide down on me, the full weight of her amazing body on my shaft.

She cried out as she slid down, her parted lips right in my face.

I stared at them as I disappeared inside her, burying myself in pulsing warmth. She was so tight I thought I might pass out.

"Oh god," she breathed. "You're so deep."

I sank my fingers into the fleshy cheeks of her ass and backed my hips up, thrusting deep against her core again.

"Fuck, Ethan."

I pressed my forehead against hers and drove inside her again, savoring how good it felt to finally fuck the girl I'd always wished was my childhood sweetheart, the girl I'd always wished was the girl next door, the only girl I would've done anything for- felt anything for- risked anything for.

She dug her fingers into my back, and I bent my legs again so I could make her feel every swollen inch of me.

I'd never been so hard for anyone.

And she was so tight I could see stars, so tight I never wanted to pull out of her, so tight I never wanted to come.

But I was going to fucking come whether I wanted to or not.

I felt her legs tighten around my waist and fucked her against the wall again, unable to hear anything except her high pitched groaning each time I buried myself inside her.

Suddenly, she pressed her cheek against mine and hugged her tits against my chest. "Take me to bed, Ethan."

I clenched my jaw as she throbbed around me and stepped away from the wall.

Then I walked around the corner and traveled the few steps to my bed, taking a knee first and then laying her down carefully without removing my dick from her incredible heat.

She looked up at me with sparkling eyes.

"Better?" I said, rocking over her.

She nodded. "You feel so good. Too good."

"So do you," I said, rocking her against the bed, her tits moving under me as I massaged her insides.

"You feel like we should've done this a long time ago," she said, her eyes on mine.

I groaned as my dick swelled. The pressure was so great I knew the dreaded end of my pleasure was near. A moment later, I felt my balls tighten as they swung against her, causing spasms of heat to shoot up my spine.

She raised her arms over her head.

I pinned her wrists down under my hands.

She scrunched her face as I sped up the pace, her expression twisting just enough that I was confident she could handle me.

And when she bit her bottom lip, I came like a cannon, emptying myself inside her in a series of heavy bursts, my eyes on hers the whole time.

When I had nothing left, I collapsed on top of her, buried my face in her neck, and struggled to catch my breath. "What have we done, Jenny," I whispered into her hair.

She wrapped her arms around my back. "Something we had to do," she said, pressing her cheek against my head.

I didn't want to pull out, didn't want the moment to end.

How could I face her again? After giving away how much I wanted her?

There was no pretending I was harmless now. There was no laughing this off.

I'd gone down on her and fucked her against the wall. I tasted every inch of her gorgeous body and sucked the breath from her mouth.

And it wasn't only physical.

It never had been.

What just went down in my bed was the nail in the mindfuck of a coffin I'd been laying in since I first saw her.

And I felt guilty about my lack of remorse, about the size of the load I'd just pumped inside her. I felt guilty that I'd undone years of trying to get over her with one fucking lick of her nipple.

She was as under my skin as I was inside her.

And there was no going back now.

She knew too much.

And I'd felt too much.

We were still totally fucked.

Only now, more than ever.

FLASHBACK
- Jenny -

It was the hottest day of the whole summer the day Brandi lied to me.

She told me that she and Ethan hooked up at a bonfire at some older girl's house.

I should've known she was full of shit. The whole story was so elaborate, and like most liars, she used too many words, adding details that weren't part of the story.

I couldn't even speak while she was talking.

After ten minutes, she stopped to ask if I wanted to know more or if I was uncomfortable.

I called her a bitch and started to cry.

That's when she hugged me and told me it wasn't true.

Then I called her a bitch a few more times and tried to dry my eyes, but it was too late.

She wanted the truth, and she got it.

"Fine," I said. "So what if I have a little crush on him? It's not like I'd do anything about it."

"I know," she said. "But other girls will, and you need to prepare yourself for that."

I didn't understand.

"Your feelings for him are way too obvious," she said.

I shook my head.

"Only to me," she said. "But if your mom suspects anything, she might separate you."

That's when I realized she was trying to do me a favor, that she wasn't actually a complete bitch. She just knew what I wanted better than I knew myself and was looking out for me. Like she always did… though I often hated her methods.

That night I sat in my window seat with an open book against my bent knees, pretending to read.

But in actual fact, I was watching Ethan shoot free throws in the driveway.

I remember being completely mesmerized by the fact that he could shoot that many times from the same place without losing interest or focus. It almost seemed like a superpower.

Shot after shot after shot for two hours.

If it hadn't gotten dark, I don't even think he would've come in.

I realized that I needed to have that kind of focus from then on.

If I was going to hide the fact that my crush on him was like a constant cramp in my side, I was going to have to practice every day, without losing interest. I'd have to train like an athlete, until I made not thinking about him look easy, until even I believed in my skill.

Otherwise, we might get separated.

I didn't even know what that would look like, what that would even mean.

I just knew I didn't want it to happen.

Because the thought of not having him around made me feel hollow.

THIRTY THREE
- Jenny -

No one ever wanted me like that.

Not even close.

There was no question that I was seduced by his desire.

From the moment I said I wouldn't ask him to stop, it was as if all of his senses were feasting on me. His longing was so tangible, so intense, I couldn't stop myself from throwing caution to the wind and inviting him to touch me.

And touch me he did.

My body always felt like something I needed to keep a secret from him, but letting him explore every inch of it with his greedy mouth and his strong hands was incredibly liberating.

From the way he sank his thick fingers into my butt cheeks to the way his lips sucked at the thin flesh on my neck, giving myself to him was the most wonderful experience of my whole life.

I just hoped it was okay for him, too.

He seemed happy enough.

And he'd fallen asleep soon after, which was supposed to be a good sign, right?

Not that I would know.

The only thing I was certain of was that I would've been tight.

After all, I'd never even had a finger in me before- besides my own of course. But that was purely out of curiosity, and I definitely hadn't fucked myself like he had.

If anything, his touch made me feel like I never knew what the hell I was doing down there.

But he certainly did.

It was different than I thought it would be, though.

I mean, I never thought he'd go down on me for one.

I thought he'd just fuck me- if I was lucky- and be done with it.

Then at least my virginity wouldn't be an issue anymore and even better, I would've lost it to the person I always wanted to lose it to.

As far as him going down on me, I guess amazing was the only word that even came close. The whole thing was so tender and sexy I couldn't believe it.

And then when he drank me down... Oh god. I could still hear the sound of him lapping at me if I closed my eyes, the sound of him groaning as his tongue splashed against my wet center.

Maybe he was right.

Maybe he was the worst stepbrother ever.

But he was by far the best lover I'd ever had- the only lover- which seemed to make the gravity of the situation even more palpable.

I laid still as I listened to him sleep.

How was I ever going to nod off with him dripping out of me like this?

I took a deep breath and let my head sink against his pillow.

Having him inside me was incredible.

There was no blood, no pain. Probably because I was ready to have sex years ago. But nobody even remotely special ever came along.

And I was under no delusions that everyone's first time was ballad worthy or anything, but I always hoped mine would at the very least be with someone I trusted, someone I was attracted to, and someone who wasn't gay. Of course, those three things were harder to find in the drama department than I anticipated.

And now I knew what I'd been missing.

But I didn't wish I'd done it sooner.

I was glad it was Ethan in the end. Except I suspected I was in big trouble now.

Because as I laid in the dark, relaxed from head to toe as I listened to the sound of his breathing beside me, I swear I could feel the crazy chemicals firing in my body.

But I had to act cool.

If anyone was sick of crazy girls getting attached too soon, it had to be him.

And I couldn't get attached.

After all, what we did wasn't okay.

I mean, obviously we were okay with it, but we couldn't just make a habit of kissing in the park and sleeping together from now on, could we?

How far across the line had we gone?

Was it even visible anymore from where we lay?

What's more, as romantic as he'd been with the flowers and the saying he always wanted this, too, there was a good chance it was just sex for him.

Perhaps I was simply the girl he couldn't have for all those years, and that was all this was about: the impossible conquest, the one that got away, the one night stand with the stepsister.

I didn't know what the fuck he was into.

I just knew I wished it were me.

And that I wasn't sorry for what I'd done. Or the fact that I deceived him to do it. After all, feeling connected to him like that was the most glorious, complete feeling I ever had.

And I really, really, really didn't want to feel bad about it.

Because I loved him.

And love wasn't bad, right?

It was supposed to be a good thing. People celebrated it every chance they got. They wrote songs and books about it. They threw big parties that nearly left them bankrupt just to prove how fantastic their love was.

But I didn't know what my love for Ethan could look like in that public space.

Maybe it was a love that had to be kept behind closed doors, in which case, had we even made any progress tonight?

He groaned and reached his arm around me, pulling my naked body against his.

I closed my eyes and relished the weight of his arm over me, scooting my bent knees back so they fit against his warm body.

I always wanted to be the little spoon.

Still, the knowledge that it was the happiest moment of my life made it difficult to enjoy.

Because I knew it couldn't last.

When we woke up in the morning, I wasn't going to be his girlfriend or his lover or his dream come true.

I'd just be his dirty little secret.

And I really believed what we had was more than that. I really believed that it wasn't dirty, that it was beautiful, and that it shouldn't have to be a secret.

It should be able to stand next to anyone else's love with its chin up and its chest out.

Sure, I was young and naïve and full of self-doubt and anxiety, but there was one thing I wasn't confused about. And that was the fact that I loved Ethan Fitzell.

I always had.

So no matter what happened, I wouldn't stop rooting for us.

Because of all my greatest hopes and most deluded ambitions, the one that inspired me most was the dream that everyday could be as wonderful as this.

THIRTY FOUR
- Ethan -

I smelled her before I even opened my eyes.

When I finally did, she was facing me, her eyes closed gently.

She looked so young when she was sleeping.

I swallowed.

What the hell was I supposed to do now?

Normally I'd treat a girl to some breakfast and get her home- if she wasn't already gone in the morning.

But I didn't know how I was going to deal with this situation.

Had I taken advantage of her?

If I had, I fucking loved it.

Did that make me an asshole?

No. She wanted it, too. She'd said so.

And I agreed with her when she said it was something we should've done a lot sooner.

Sleeping with her was more than I ever dreamed it would be. Hell, having her body in my hands and wrapped around me was the greatest thrill of my life.

How long had I wanted that? Ten years?

No, not quite that long. But only because I didn't realize I wanted her like that in the beginning.

It was more harmless then.

I was merely curious about the girl that sang to herself on the bus, the girl with the freckles and the 3D sweaters. I didn't know I wanted her sexually at the time.

But knew I did now, and I couldn't shake the feeling that that complicated things.

After all, I didn't feel that safe indifference I usually felt the morning after, that comforting confidence that no matter what, the woman I was lying next to had wanted it more than I had.

On the contrary, I felt infatuated. Obsessed. Sick.

What the hell was wrong with me?

This was what I always wanted, wasn't it?

No.

What I always wanted was her, and I still didn't have that.

Because while last night answered some questions, it raised even more of them.

The first one being: what fucking next?

Could this continue?

I wanted it to. Fuck the consequences. I didn't need other women like I needed her.

But Jen deserved better. She deserved a guy she could go out with and introduce to her friends, a guy who could walk down the red carpet with her without causing a fucking Angelina-Jolie-brother-kissing-tabloid-nightmare.

And no matter how strong my feelings for her were, I couldn't believe that she would risk everything to be with me.

Even if she could tell her friends, what about our parents?

My dad would probably treat me like a worthless piece of shit, but that was the least of my concerns. His judgements for me had been so numerous over the years that they held little weight now.

But Jenny and her mom were close. If she thought for one second her mom would disown her for this shit, we didn't have a chance.

God I wished I could know what was in her head without fucking discussing it.

Discussing it never helped.

Shit. That's why I suggested we put it off last night. Overthinking things was never the answer.

But neither was burying my head in the sand.

Or her pussy if I was lucky.

And boy was I.

Last night had been a dream come true.

And now that dream was laying a foot away from me, naked in my bed.

Maybe we could elope?

Maybe we could start anew somewhere else, somewhere these bullshit labels wouldn't follow us or hold up in court.

I exhaled slowly. I had to chill out.

It didn't matter how much I wanted her and how much I was willing to risk to be with her.

What mattered was what she wanted, and until I knew that, there was no point in dwelling on the situation.

After all, she could've been using me.

She could've shown up here in the hope of crashing at my place and indulging in some teenage fantasy, and that might be the end of it. I didn't know. I hadn't seen her in years.

Of course, now I'd seen all of her.

And despite everything, I wanted to see it all again.

I slid backwards out of the bed, stood up, grabbed a pair of boxers from my dresser, and headed to the bathroom.

After I took a piss, I looked in the mirror. My mind flashed back to how it felt to have her fingernails digging into my back, her eyes on my abs. On my dick.

If she weren't my stepsister, I'd be trying to figure out how soon I could take her out again and get her lips around my dick.

I shuddered at the thought.

I didn't want to have those thoughts about her- and yet I couldn't help myself.

I was like an addict who'd had a hit, and all I could think about was my next one.

Fuck rehab and fuck all my hard work. I had to get inside that girl again no matter what.

I flicked the lights off and opened the door.

Jenny had rolled over so she was facing the bathroom, and she made a satisfied little groaning noise when she saw me through her half open eyes. "Hey stranger."

I'd never wanted to be a stranger so bad in my life. "Hey," I said, sitting on the edge of the bed.

She reached a hand around to my lower back and dragged her nails along the base of my spine. "How did you sleep?"

"Good," I said, admiring the sexy way her mascara had smudged around her eyes. "You?"

"Good," she said. "But-"

I furrowed my brow. "But what?"

"It's like I can still feel you inside me," she said, casting her eyes down towards her lap.

"What do you mean?"

"I mean-" She pursed her lips. "Can I tell you something?"

"Anything. Of course."

"I never did that before."

"Tell me about it."

"No, I mean, never. With anyone."

I craned my neck forward. "What?"

"Don't make me say it. I feel awkward enough."

I scooted away from her. "What have you never done?"

"I've never been with anyone like that."

My eyes grew wide. "Why didn't you stop me?"

She shrugged. "For the same reason you didn't stop me."

I shook my head. "That's not okay, Jenny."

"I wanted it to be you," she said. "What does it matter?"

I rubbed my hands over my face.

"I thought you'd be flattered."

Fuck.

"Forget it. Pretend I never said anything."

I swallowed. "How could you not tell me that?"

"Cause I didn't want you to change your mind about being with me."

I clenched my jaw. "Are you sure?"

She squinted at me. "Am I sure I was a virgin till last night?"

I felt a dark pit sprout in my stomach.

I didn't know what to think.

It was one thing to think her heart was vulnerable and that she'd given it to me for the night, but it was quite another to realize the extent of her body's naivety and know how completely she'd trusted me with it.

"Ethan- say something."

I scoffed and got up. "You mean like you should've last night?"

And then I walked out of the room.

Because that's what I always did when I was in over my head.

THIRTY FIVE
- Jenny -

"What the fuck, Ethan?!"

I jumped out of the bed before I remembered I was completely naked. "Don't walk away from me when we're-" I reached for the bathroom door, grabbed his robe off the hook, and threw it on as I scrambled after him.

When I walked into the main room, he was scooping coffee into the filter. "Should I not have said anything?" I laid my hands on the counter. "Okay, don't answer that. Obviously I should've mentioned it, but-"

He didn't look at me. He just stuck the pot on its stand, flicked the orange button, and kept his back to me.

"Ethan, please."

He turned around with crossed arms. "What you should've done was lose it to somebody else. Anybody else."

I felt like he'd taken a dagger to my guts. How could he say something like that? Wasn't it a nice surprise? Especially if you'd done everything right like he did?

"No wonder you asked me to take you to bed." He threw his hands in the air. "What woman wants to lose it to some guy against a random wall?"

He looked so cold standing in the kitchen in his boxers, his bare feet on the tile.

"You're not some guy," I said, reaching towards the basket of freshly folded laundry by the door. I flipped through the stack and threw him some sweatpants as soon as I found a pair.

While he put them on, I walked back around to the other side of the counter. "I thought we had a good time."

"Me too," he said. "Until I found out we weren't having the same time. You had an agenda and you used me."

"No-" I wrapped a hand around my eyes.

"And somehow I'm the one who feels like a goddamn user. Like I took advantage of you-"

"But I wanted you to!"

"How is it even possible that you've never had sex before? You just graduated from college for fuck's sake."

I cocked my head. "What the hell is that supposed to mean?"

He reached for the cupboard and pulled out one mug.

"Well?" His robe was down to my ankles, and I pulled the navy fleece around me, wishing I were in those cozy socks he let me borrow the other day. Then at least one small part of me would feel comfortable right now. "Not everyone sleeps around."

The glowing orange coffee button flicked off, and he pulled the pot from the stand. "I just assumed-"

I watched him fill the mug with coffee. "What?"

"I assumed you would've ticked that milestone off a long time ago." He leaned forward and set the mug down in front of me. Then he went back to get one for himself.

"Me too," I said, wrapping my palms around the hot mug. "But it didn't happen, and I didn't want to force it with some random person I didn't trust."

"But Brandi's-"

I furrowed my brow. "What?"

"You know."

"I'm afraid I don't," I lied. "And just because my best friend's more experienced than I am doesn't-"

"You went to prom with that rattlesnake Tom Denic."

"Yeah, I did," I said. "On your dad's condition that I be home by eleven thirty."

He clenched his jaw.

"Which was my curfew until I went to college by the way. And don't get me wrong, there were other kids getting drunk and fucked before eleven, but I wasn't one of them."

He raised both hands and rubbed his temples.

"You know he used to breathalyze me?"

He lifted his gaze.

"And make me run through self-defense drills?"

His eyes grew wide.

"And while I never knew for sure, I always assumed there was some kind of tracking device on the car-"

"I could've told you that," he said. "Along with how to get it off."

I folded my arms. "The point is, the opportunity was rarely there, and even if it had been, it's not like I was going to lose it to Tom Denic." I shuddered. Even the thought of getting fingered by someone who bit their cuticles like that made me feel seedy.

"Okay, I get it. I know my dad's a tyrant, and to be honest, it only got worse after my mom died so I'm not surprised he made your life hell."

I shook my head. "He didn't. I mean, yeah, at the time I thought he was trying to ruin my life, but what did I really miss out on? A few drinking tickets? Running from the cops? Getting felt up by drunk members of the marching band? If anything, I owe him one."

Ethan raised his eyebrows.

"Don't tell him I said that, though."

"And college?" he asked. "Surely there were assholes lining up to take you out."

I shrugged. "There were, I guess. Or at least there were more opportunities. But after waiting so long, I didn't want my first time to be with some guy who tasted like Jager and didn't even know my last name."

"Uh-huh."

"Plus, I was a drama major."

"So?"

"So most of my male friends are gay, and frankly, wine nights playing Cards of Humanity don't get quite that raunchy." I took a sip of my coffee and stared at him over the top of my mug.

He was backed in the far corner of the kitchen.

I felt awful that he wanted to be so far away from me after holding me all night. "I'm sorry, okay?"

He sighed.

"I should've told you."

His face was stony.

"You had a right to know."

He scoffed.

"But for what it's worth, I don't have any regrets about it."

"Was it-"

"What?"

"Okay?" He raised his eyebrows. "I mean, for your first time?"

I swallowed.

"Cause I can't help but feel I should've been more gentle-"

I shook my head. "It was perfect."

"And you always wanted it to be me?"

I nodded. "Yeah. I did. Despite everything."

"What do you mean despite everything?"

"Despite our parents," I said, squeezing the warm mug in my hands. "And you being such an asshole to me ever since they got together."

"I wasn't an asshole."

"I'm pretty sure you were. I used to cry about it and everything."

He leaned off the counter. "What?"

"You used to make fun of me and tell me I was a weirdo-"

"I never-"

"Yeah, you did. You used to tell me my sweaters were lame and that my friends were losers and ask me why I couldn't try harder to fit in or get a boyfriend or listen to better music or-"

"Okay, I get it. I was an asshole."

I pursed my lips and let it sink in, let him stare at the floor tiles and feel bad about it like I used to. But in reality, he probably did me a favor because his bad behavior helped mitigate the miserable, aching desire I had for him at the time.

And he never once criticized me in front of anyone else. Not once.

Sure, I used to be bothered by his teasing, by the cutting tone of his voice when he put me down. But I still preferred those moments to when we were in public and he wouldn't even acknowledge me.

And now I'd lost my virginity to him.

Just like I always wanted.

So I guess he was right.

I was a total weirdo.

THIRTY SIX
- Ethan -

I hadn't felt this fucked in the head since I was seventeen... though the first night Jen showed up at my place was a close second.

There I was with a fucking hard on and her suddenly in my living room. That was a bit of a shock.

And now I found myself staring at her from across the kitchen- where she stood wrapped in nothing but my robe with her bedhead falling everywhere- and I was just as clueless as to what to do.

On one hand, my chest was swollen with pride that she'd always wanted it to be me.

However, I spent the guts of the last decade trying not to get attached to her, and this news didn't help.

Knowing I was the only man she'd given herself to like that only made me feel more possessive and infatuated with her. And sick. Mostly I felt sick. Like nauseous and lightheaded and uncharacteristically anxious.

And try as I might, it was hard not to think those symptoms were a direct result of how hard I'd let myself fall.

Granted, I had enough self-awareness that I kind of knew it was happening at the time, but I thought I'd be able to pick myself up, dust myself off, and say goodbye to her when all was said and done. But I was starting to think it wasn't going to be that easy.

After all, where would that leave me?

Worse off than ever, I assume. Because while it was one thing to never get what you want, surely losing that thing once you've had it is a pain worse than death.

In fact, maybe that's what was causing me to feel so ill: the knowledge that this dream could all come to an end in the time it took her to drag her suitcase out of my building.

"I'm sorry," I said, adding some hot coffee to my cup.

She raised her eyebrows.

"For being an asshole all those years." I walked over, topped her up, and set the coffee pot down between us. "And for making you cry."

She shrugged. "Everything made me cry back then."

"I know. I remember. But still."

"Hormones," she said. "What a mindfuck, eh?"

I nodded. "Testosterone certainly got me into a lot of trouble."

She lowered her head. "Does this mean you forgive me? For not telling you I was a virgin."

"What choice do I have?"

"I don't get what the problem is? What are you so afraid of?"

I took a deep breath.

"Are you afraid I'll latch onto you like a barnacle and refuse to let go?"

If anything, I was afraid she wouldn't.

"That I'll go crazy and get jealous and start stalking you or something?"

I blinked at her. She didn't even know the meaning of jealousy as far as I was concerned.

"Is that what you think happens when girls lose their virginity? Because I hate to break it to you, but not everyone mates for life."

I sighed.

"In fact, that would be a disaster in most of my friend's cases-"

"I'm not afraid of any of those things."

She raised her eyebrows. "What is it then? Because you've been acting like a freak all morning."

I dropped my head and stared into my coffee.

"And I was a freak for a long time so I know a freak out when I see one-"

"I'm afraid of falling in love with you."

Her lips fell apart.

"And for the record, it's not the love part that scares me," I said. "It's the you part."

She pursed her lips.

"Because our being together is impossible, but my falling for you isn't."

She blinked at me.

"To be honest, that's what I've always been afraid of."

She shook her head.

"I was so afraid of it I left."

"No."

"Yes."

"That's not true. You left because you frightened Aaron Schwartz so bad he peed himself in front of the whole locker room."

I nodded. "Yeah. And I did it because of what he was saying about you."

"What?"

I shrugged.

"Then why didn't you-"

"What? Repeat what he said to the principal and degrade you when he already got what he deserved?"

She raised a finger, her eyes glassy. "Don't put that on me. Don't say it's my fault you left. I didn't want you to go."

I reached across the counter and forced her finger down. "I'm not putting anything on you. I'm just telling you what happened."

She swallowed. "What did he say?"

I shook my head. "It doesn't matter-"

"Ethan."

"I don't rememb-"

"Tell me."

"He was just being vulgar and saying stuff about your lips."

She pursed them.

I stared as she let them reappear.

She cocked her head. "You stood up for me?"

"I wasn't gonna let him talk about you like that."

"But you went away for it." She craned her neck forwards. "You let everyone think you were some kind of troubled, angry teen."

"I was."

She shook her head. "I don't believe that. I don't think you needed help."

"I did," I said. "I couldn't process my mom's death there. I had to get away."

"You could've gotten help."

"Trust me. I've thought a lot about this."

She dropped her head and stared at the steam rising from her mug.

"There are only two things that could've helped me get through it, and I wasn't free to choose either of them." I walked around the counter and stepped up beside her.

"I hoped you would come back," she whispered, turning to me so I could see the tear pooling on her lower lid. "Your leaving punished me, too, ya know?"

I lifted a hand to her cheek. "It wasn't you I left, Jenny."

She put a hand over mine and pressed it to her face.

"I left my problems. And my anger. But not you." I leaned forward and kissed her on the forehead.

She laid a hand against my chest.

"I've got to go to work this afternoon," I said, leaning back to catch her eye. "You okay to do you for a while?"

She nodded. "Yeah."

"What do you want to do about us in the meantime?"

She shrugged. "Keep it a secret, I guess."

I raised my eyebrows.

"Like it's always been."

I forced a smile. "Whatever you want."

I walked into the bathroom and leaned my back against the door, the pit in my stomach aching.

My feelings for her were too big to be a secret, and I already knew it.

I just didn't know what the fuck to do about it.

THIRTY SEVEN
- Jenny -

I remember the day he left.

I gave him the most awkward hug of my adolescent life and then refused to go along to the train station with our parents to wave him off.

Instead, I stayed home and cried, indulging myself in how betrayed I felt that he would abandon me like that.

Of course, part of me was angry that he'd gotten out when I was still stuck with our obnoxiously smitten parents in a town full of people who were so dull they'd never even been to Columbus, much less out of state.

I cried until there was nothing left.

Then I wrote him an angry letter, confessing all my feelings and admitting that I never hated him, not even for one second. Then I tore it into tiny little pieces and threw it in six different garbage cans the next day at school.

I thought that would get him out of my system, thought I could purge the feelings that way and not have to feel them anymore.

I remember the first day at school when I didn't overhear his name a single time. It was only a week and a half later. I remember feeling disgusted that everyone could just move on like that and forget him. It was the first time I was glad my angry letter shredding voodoo hadn't worked.

And all that because he was defending me.

I couldn't believe it.

No wonder Aaron Schwartz never so much as looked in my direction again. It all made sense. Ethan had threatened him. Thoroughly. Shit, it was probably partly his fault I never got laid in high school.

I had just crossed into the park when I felt my phone buzz against my hip. I waited until I had a little bit of personal space- and until I knew I was headed in the right direction- before hitting the callback button.

"Oh my god," Brandi said. "Please tell me you're a huge star already and in desperate need of a cleaning lady to destroy the evidence from all your massive coke parties."

"Uhhh."

"Cause I've got to get out of this town."

"Why? What happened now?"

"I got recognized by a cab driver yesterday."

"So?"

"He recognized me because I left swiped him on Tinder."

I smiled. "That could only happen to you."

"Me and Amy Schumer I like to think."

"What did you do?"

"Got dropped off on Maple, obviously, so he wouldn't know where the fuck I lived."

"I told you to stop using Tinder when you got home from school. Our town is way too small. Next thing you know you'll be swiping married guys and former teachers."

"If Mr. Crawford popped up, I'd totally right swipe."

"You're disgusting."

"What's disgusting is what I'd teach him about biology."

"Stop. I can't listen to this. I had him for homeroom."

She laughed. "Does that mean you won't come to the wedding?"

"What wedding? The one between Ted and Brandi Crawford? Not a chance in hell."

She sighed. "Fine. Save me from my sad teacher student fantasy."

"I can't. You're obviously in too deep." I moved to the side of the path to avoid a squirrel and an oncoming biker.

"At least tell me things are heating up between you and Ethan."

I scrunched my face. "Define heating up."

"Has he put his hands on you yet?"

I didn't want to encourage her line of questioning. "We went to dinner last night."

"Somewhere fancy?"

"Yeah. With real bruschetta and everything."

"Wow. What was the occasion?"

"Me being in New York, I guess."

"And then?"

"And then after a lot of white wine he kissed me in the park."

She squealed.

I held the phone away from my ear.

"How was it?" she asked.

"Too good," I said. "The best ever."

"You guys are freaks. What would your parents say?"

"Well, I'm pretty sure his dad would disown him and he wouldn't care."

"And your mom?"

I sighed. "I don't think she'd understand. I think she'd think I was rebelling or something."

"No offense, but you're a pretty shitty rebel."

"I always thought so, too. Until last night."

"Did anything else happen?"

"No," I lied. "But I think something could. If I wanted."

"Whoa."

"I know."

"So is it too early for you to tell me I was totally right about you guys having the hots for each other?"

"No. It seems you were right, but would you mind keeping it to yourself until I figure out what the heck is going on?"

"Sure. But only because I know that kind of juicy gossip would spread like wildfire around here."

"And you are literally the only person who knows besides Ethan, and he's not going to tell anybody."

"Your secret is safe with me."

"Good."

"But only if you tell me what really happened."

I ran a hand over my head. "I told you."

"You expect me to believe that he kissed you and stopped there? After all those years of jacking off to the thought of your-"

"Brandi!"

"Sorry, but you know I'm right."

I groaned.

"I don't know the guy that well, but he never struck me as the tender kiss goodnight type."

"There may have been a bit of harmless fooling around once we got home, but that's it."

"That's it?"

"Yeah."

"You are full of shit, but I know this is a crazy big deal for you so I'm going to give you some time to make sense of it."

"Thank you."

"But then I expect every last detail."

"Deal," I said. "And I really appreciate your support."

"And my keeping my mouth shut."

"Right."

"So now what?" she asked.

"Now I'm headed to go meet some agent Ethan got me an appointment with."

"Oh, that's exciting."

"I'm not really sure what to expect," I said. "Hopefully I'll get to meet the guy, but there's a chance I'll just drop off my head shots and my resume and that'll be it."

"I'll keep my fingers crossed for you."

"Thanks."

"What are you going to do if you fall for him for real?"

"The agent? I don't think–"

"Not the agent, dummy. Ethan."

I pursed my lips. "I don't know. I can't figure out if that would be the worst thing ever or the best."

"Probably depends on who you ask."

"No shit," I said. "Why do you ask?"

"I don't know. I guess part of me likes to believe that you guys would've been high school sweethearts if things had worked out differently."

"I'm sure we wouldn't have been. I was a drama geek, remember? And he was a jock."

"I know, but that's just how other people made sense of you back then. I think you guys could've overcome that, ya know? If your parents hadn't gotten in the way."

"We'll never know, will we?"

"The point is, I just want you to know you have my support," she said. "To fight for what you want."

"Uh-huh."

"And if that's more time with Ethan, I think you should go for it."

"Okaayy. Where is this coming from?"

"I think he's the only guy that ever looked at you right."

"What?"

"You deserve a guy that worships you, Jen."

"And you think Ethan is that guy?"

"I think he could be," she said. "If you stop making excuses for why he can't be."

THIRTY EIGHT
- Ethan -

I remember what she was wearing the day I left- a pair of rubber duck pajama pants and an old sweatshirt she used to wear inside out because she didn't like to feel like a walking ad for clothing brands.

She hugged me before I left, but I got the sense it was under duress. Like she only did it because our parents were standing there, and it seemed like the right thing to do. She smelled like nail polish remover.

Once my luggage was in the car, there wasn't much space. But if she'd wanted, she could've scrunched in next to me in the back of my dad's pre-owned Chevy. Instead, she stayed home.

I didn't see her for two years after that, but there wasn't a day that went by when I didn't think about her.

I even stole a picture of her from one of the shoe boxes at the bottom of the hall closet.

It was her squinting into the sun and blowing on a white dandelion. I used to guess at what she was wishing. Sometimes I would pretend it was for me to come back, even though it was taken long before I left.

I don't know why I was so fixated on her, even after I moved so far away.

Perhaps it was because she was the first beautiful thing I saw after my mom died. So I clung to her smile, her freckles, her chiming laugh, as if they were symbols that life could go on...

The day she died was the first and last day I ever waterskied.

The sun was as bright as I'd ever seen it that Saturday morning when we arrived at a family friend's lake house. My mom loved the lake, along with the ocean, rivers, rain... any kind of water really.

I used to love going to the lake, too, because I'd get to eat hot dogs and Fritos all weekend- and lots of barbequed corn, which I always believed was unfairly classified as a vegetable.

I used to struggle getting up on the skis. I found it nerve wracking and difficult, but that day I finally did it.

And once I got the hang of it, I couldn't get enough. I was crushing it. Best of all, my parents and the Toohey's were cheering me on big time. I can still recall how proud I was to see them all clapping and waving at me from the back of the boat.

Eventually, I needed a rest and it was my mom's turn to go out next. She was really good. She could lift one ski up and jump in the air. It was one of the only things I can remember her being a show off at.

As soon as she let go, Mr. Toohey hit the brakes and started to turn the boat around so we could pick her up and see if she wanted to go again.

And that's when those idiots came tearing around the corner straight towards her.

We all waved our arms and yelled for them to slow down.

But they weren't even paying attention. They were shitfaced and going too fast and she was just in the wrong place at the wrong time.

If I'd gone for one more spin it might've been me.

My dad pulled her out of the water.

She was unconscious and bleeding from the side of her head. It wasn't until years later that I realized she was lucky she didn't lose her head completely.

The postmortem said she was killed instantly, and that even if she hadn't been, her brain never could've survived the impact.

The driver lost his boating license and a few years of his life to jail.

I lost my mom.

"You okay?" Woody asked as he handed me a crate of Bacardi from the back of an open truck.

"Yeah," I said. "Just a little down."

"You want to talk about it?"

"I suppose if I did, you'd be the guy to talk to."

"Sure would," he said. "I've just about been through it all."

"What do you know about loss, Woody?"

Woody sat down on the end of the truck bed and checked his watch.

None of the other staff were due to arrive for another hour, which was more time than we needed to unload the truck.

"What kind of loss are we talking about?" he asked, sliding the last crate my way. "Because I know what it's like to lose your home, your parents, your self-belief, even your marbles."

I forced a smile and put the last crate on the trolley. I had no right to sulk around Woody.

The guy had been homeless before Ben gave him a job here, and he'd taken the opportunity with both hands and turned his life around in the space of a year.

"I lost my mom when I was a kid," I said. "It was a boating accident. She died instantly, and I saw it happen."

He nodded. "I'm sorry, Ethan. That's fucked up."

"Yeah, even after all this time."

"My mom was a junkie. She died in an empty bathtub after shooting up between her toes."

"Shit."

"I like to think she felt good on the way out."

I tilted my head. "Didn't you feel kind of abandoned?"

"Yes and no."

I raised my eyebrows.

He pulled his chin where his thick beard used to be. "Yes, because I was on my own after that, hopping between foster homes like a frog hops between lily pads."

"Yeah."

"But no because she didn't owe me anything, ya know? She never asked for me. I was just one more thing that happened to her in her life, if that makes sense."

"Sort of." I leaned an elbow on the inside of the truck.

"There are two kinds of people in this world, Ethan."

"Go on."

"People who stuff happens to, and people who make stuff happen."

I nodded.

"And I've been both," he said, sliding down from the truck bed. "And I can tell you, the latter's where it's at."

I stepped back so we could close and latch the doors.

"Stuff used to happen to me," he said. "And I used to let it be an excuse for why I couldn't get this or that or go after this or learn that or-"

"Got it."

"But stuff happens to everybody." He grabbed the front handle on the trolley.

I pressed two hands against the crates at the back to keep them steady while he pulled.

"So your stuff isn't an excuse," he said. "Unless you want it to be. But then you end up being one of those people life happens to."

"A victim."

"Yeah." He switched the hand he was pulling with.

"So what changed for you?" I asked. "After all those years on the streets?"

He shrugged. "I just started dwelling on my moments of good fortune instead of my moments of bad."

"Something tells me you're simplifying things."

"Sure I am," he said. "But it's easy to overcomplicate stuff, and you don't get any extra points in the end for making life harder than it needs to be."

"I suppose that's true."

He smacked a flat button beside the double doors so we could wheel the stock into the club's storeroom. "So whatever it is that's got you down," he said. "My advice is to shake it off."

I took a deep breath.

"Because when you focus on what's got you down, you can't see all the reasons you have to get up."

"And what if you can't have what you want?"

He walked backwards for a moment and squinted at me. "Why wouldn't you be able to have what you want?"

I shrugged. "Cause life isn't fair."

He scoffed. "Life's plenty fair," he said. "Or at least, it's the same kind of fair for everyone."

"Perhaps."

"So unless you want something that's going to bring harm to someone else, you ought to go after it."

"I suppose."

"You suppose right, Ethan," he said, fixing his eyes on me. "After all, the worst thing that can happen is you fail."

"Right."

"And failing can be tough, but there's no failure like not trying."

THIRTY NINE
- Jenny -

I'd never seen so many skinny girls and moody looking boys.

It was the first time in my life I felt like I should've colored in my eyebrows and worn Spanx.

"Jennifer Layne?" A woman at the front of the waiting room stared down at her clipboard. How her thin frames stayed on her nose was beyond me.

I stood up and lifted a palm towards her as two dozen eyes watched me like the hungry cast of a perfume commercial.

The woman led me down a narrow hallway which was lined with black and white headshots of glamourous people with bedroom eyes. Then she opened a door at the end of the hall and nodded for me to enter.

A man with a sizeable pot belly concealed under his blue button down sat behind the cherry wood desk along the far wall.

I heard the door close behind me.

"Jennifer-" He looked from me to a paper on his desk. "Layne, is it?"

I nodded.

"I was expecting you to be more butch."

I raised my eyebrows. "Excuse me?"

"My nephew was under the impression that you were bald. And gay."

My lips fell apart.

"Not that there's anything wrong with either of those things, but I wasn't expecting a full head of hair."

I tilted an ear towards him. "I'm not gay either."

He squinted at me. "Not even a little bit?" he asked. "Because there's a huge demand for-"

"I'm not a homophobe or anything," I said. "I would take a gay role if that's what you're asking. If it was tasteful. I have gay frien-"

"Forget it," he said, standing and walking around his desk with a swagger that suggested heavy shoes. "It's obviously a misunderstanding."

I swallowed and took a step forward. The room was beige and bare apart from a few movie posters on the walls between the windows.

"Ira," he said, sticking out a chubby hand.

I took it. "Thanks for agreeing to meet me on such short notice."

"No problem." He nodded at the manila folder in my hand. "Is that for me?"

I handed to him. "It is."

"Great. Have a seat, Jenny, and we'll get right down to it."

I bent my legs and balanced on the edge of the chair, suddenly conscious of my posture after seeing all the swan necks in the waiting room.

He sat down with such force that his chair rolled back several inches. "So I take it you're from a small town in the middle of the country that no one's ever heard of and you want to be a star."

I scrunched my face. "Would you prefer if I made up a more original story?"

"Not at all," he said. "Everyone loves that one, but I appreciate you offering." He laid the folder down in front of him and flipped it open.

I pursed my lips, watched his dark eyes scan the stack of pictures accompanying my resume, and listened to his heavy breathing as I prayed he'd be able to help me.

"What's your dream role?" he asked, lifting his eyes. "If I could snap my fingers and have you cast in something tomorrow."

"Norma in Sunset Boulevard."

He nodded and stuck his lower lip out. "So you're a confident singer?"

"Very."

He leaned back in his chair, folded his hands over his stomach, and nodded.

I raised my eyebrows. "You want me to sing something?"

"Well, I can't send you somewhere to sing with my recommendation if I haven't heard you, now can I?" He shook his head. "No offense, but you wouldn't believe the shit people lie to me about- that they tap dance, that they do their own stunts, that they'll take their clothes off when they won't, that their sex change is complete-"

"I understand."

"Great." He nodded. "When you're ready."

I took a deep breath.

"That means now."

I started singing Norma's big song from Sunset Boulevard with all the feeling I could. And it was easy. I'd cried to "With One Look" a thousand times.

He kept his eyes on me and let me sing the first four stanzas, raising his hand to stop me after I sang the part about making the whole world cry.

"Good."

I smiled, relieved to have sung out some of my nervous energy.

"In forty years, you'll be a great Norma."

"Thank you."

"But let's see if we can get you something more age appropriate in the meantime."

I raised my eyebrows.

"There are auditions next week for Chicago. A few of the main parts are already spoken for, but in my opinion, what you need is some exposure so people with pull start to recognize your name. At this stage, even snagging a role as a stand in would be a worthwhile victory for you."

"I completely agree," I said. "I'm not so naive that I think I'm going to be Elphaba by next summer. I'm open to anything and willing to put in all the hard work it takes."

"Is this all your updated contact information?" he asked, pointing at the page in front of him.

I nodded.

"Great," he said. "Now, before you get your hopes up, I can't promise you anything."

"I know."

"But I'll do what I can to make sure a few people see you in the next few weeks as a favor to my nephew."

"Sure."

"And if people like you and you get some work, we can draw up something official."

"Something official?"

He waved his hands in the air. "Yeah. Something that says it's my job to lose sleep over making sure you get jobs in this city."

I smiled. "That sounds good."

"I thought it might."

"What should I do in the meantime?"

"Wait by the phone," he said. "I'll be in touch in the next forty eight hours."

"Great."

"Other than that, just make sure you don't get fat or injured or lose your voice, and we won't have any problems."

I pursed my lips and nodded.

"You can see yourself out?" he asked, raising his eyebrows.

"Yes, thank you. It was very nice to meet you."

"You, too, Jennifer. Happy to help."

I stepped out of the room and let out an exhale so big I was surprised I didn't deflate entirely. Then I did a little happy dance, shaking my hips back and forth silently for a second to help me calm down.

But I still couldn't even get close to keeping a straight face as I walked out of the office, my head held high and my chest bursting with pride.

After all, I was finally starting to feel like this city was beginning to love me back.

And there were so many people that I needed to thank for encouraging me to keep going after my dream.

But there was one person in particular that I couldn't wait to share the good news with.

FORTY
- Ethan -

Ben walked across the empty club with his keys in hand.

By the time he sat down at the bar, I'd made two Dirty Shirley's.

"I feel good about how that meeting went," he said.

I nodded. "So does everyone else, Boss."

He shrugged. "The bonuses had to happen. Things are going so well. I couldn't not incentivize people, could I?"

"You could," I said, hopping over the bar and taking a seat beside him. "But then you'd be like every other prick with a club on this street."

"You'd know."

"Sure would," I said, sliding my drink towards me. "Worked for half of 'em."

"Everything cool with your sister?" he asked. "After the other day?"

I swallowed.

"And your two nights off work?"

"Stepsister."

"Whatever."

I glanced down at my drink. "Gretchen seemed bummed that I showed up for the team meeting."

"Gretchen wants your job."

I raised my eyebrows. "I hope you told her she couldn't have it."

He shrugged. "I'm going to create a position for her. She's the closest thing to your equal we've got."

"As long as it isn't my position."

"So?" he asked, using his straw to scoop one of his cherries up from the bottom of his glass.

"So things have been better."

He furrowed his brow. "Why's that? Demons from your greedy margarita night still catching up with you?"

I shook my head. "More like I'm having the kind of problem you had with Carrie a year ago."

He craned his neck forward. "You in love or something?"

"That would be admitting the problem."

He smacked me on the arm. "Holy shit, man. Who's the lucky girl?"

"Promise you won't judge me or fire me or tell Christophe?"

He cocked his head. "Why? Is it that girl who dances at the Pussy Cat Lounge?"

I furrowed my brow. "No, Jesus. That was a one time thing."

"Gotcha."

"And I only went there cause she had that crazy tongue piercing-"

"Ribbed for your pleasure, if my memory serves."

I wrapped my hand around my forehead.

"So who is it?" he asked.

"You know how I've been entertaining a visitor this week?"

"Your sister?"

"She's my stepsister, Christ. She's as much my fucking sister as Ella is your mom."

He leaned back. "Whoa, okay. So not your sister at all."

"No."

"Zero blood relation."

I gripped my glass. "Zilch."

"How long have you guys-"

I sighed. "What?"

"Not been related?"

I rolled my eyes. "I was sixteen when our parents got married. And I got shipped off to boarding school the next year."

"For being an asshole?"

"Yeah." I nodded. "But I liked her before that."

"Wow."

"I just couldn't do anything about it before."

"And now you can? Because…?"

I pointed at him. "Exactly. That fucking 'because dot dot dot' is what's doing my head in."

"I guess I can see how your parents wouldn't be thrilled, but it seems to me there's only two things to consider."

I raised my eyebrows.

"Is this just about your dick wanting what it shouldn't?"

"Right."

He smiled. "You deviant you."

"Fuck off."

"Cause if that's what's plaguing you, man, you should probably kick her the fuck out and not go there."

"I know."

"Nobody wants a messy night of sex following them around for the rest of their life. I mean, can you imagine planning your wedding and turning to your fiancée, like, 'I won't invite anyone I've fucked raw, baby, except for my stepsister. She's cool.'"

I swiveled my stool away from him and faced forwards.

"You get what I'm saying?"

"Yeah. Don't worry. You're not that subtle."

"But there's always that second possibility," he said.

"Which is?"

"Which is that the reason the itch in your pants for this girl hasn't gone away after all this time is because she really means something to you."

I clenched my jaw.

"In which case, I'd say this sounds like one of those times it's probably better to beg for forgiveness than ask for permission."

I furrowed my brow. "I'm listening."

"That's all. I just wouldn't even waste my breath asking for my dad's blessing or my mom's or whatever the situation is-"

"Her mom and my dad."

"Right. I just wouldn't mention it until I felt like I could go to them and say, 'I fucking love this girl and it doesn't concern you.'"

"Mmm."

"As opposed to, 'I know she's my stepsister, but I just want to dip my dick in for a second to see if it fit-"

"Ben! Fuck!"

He laughed. "Sorry. I just started to picture it in my head, and it was so funny I couldn't help but-"

"Enough."

He drank some of his drink and licked his lips. "You really want to know what I think?"

"I don't know. Do I? It's been pretty scary so far."

"I think this is the first time I've ever seen you like this."

I glared at him. "Seen me like what?"

"Sprung? Confused? Sick in love?"

"I do feel fucking dreadful."

"Not a good sign you're coming out of this single, buddy."

I swiveled back towards him. "Did you feel sick when you first got with Carrie?"

He nodded. "I thought I was dying."

"Jesus. That's awful."

"Yeah, it was."

I raised my eyebrows. "How long did it last?"

"Until she was mine."

"What do you mean until she was yours?"

"I mean as soon as I knew she wanted me just as bad as I wanted her and that we weren't going to have to play any more games or waste any more time guessing what the other person was thinking, I started to feel better."

"Started?!"

"And once we moved in together, things got even better."

"That helped?"

"Are you kidding?" he asked. "As far as I'm concerned that's like the ultimate show of loyalty."

I squinted at him.

"It's like… not only am I thinking about you all the fucking time, but I'm so crazy about you that I don't even want personal space anymore."

"That's the cheesiest thing I've ever heard. What about all the toilet seat stuff and the hairs in the bathtub crap most couples bitch about?"

He shrugged. "I can't speak for other couples. I just know how I feel, and that's a whole lot better when my woman is around."

I scrunched my face. "Do you have to call her your woman? Like you're fucking James Brown?"

"Would now be a bad time to sing sex machine?"

"Yes," I said, putting my head in my hands.

He slapped me across the back. "I think this is good, Ethan. I think you'll get through this."

I swiveled around and leaned my back against the bar. "How do you figure?"

"Because if you didn't care about this girl, you wouldn't be doing this to yourself."

"Perhaps."

"And if she didn't care about you, you wouldn't be doing this to yourself."

"No?"

He shook his head. "You're too vain and comfortable being single. If you didn't think she had the potential to ruin all that for you, you wouldn't give it a second thought."

"And you're saying this sick feeling in my guts- this black knot of anxiety- that I feel growing inside me is a good thing?"

He smiled. "I'm saying that if you give it a chance to grow, it might just be the best thing that ever happened to you."

FORTY ONE
- Jenny -

I was bursting to tell Ethan the good news.

Hopefully, his obvious weirdness had passed.

Not that he didn't have a right to freak out. I mean, our behavior was questionable, and I did lie by omission. Still, now was the worst time for him to push me away.

I unlocked his apartment door and was about to call his name when I noticed that the mystery door was ajar.

My heart pounded in my chest as I approached it, bracing myself for what I might find.

When I peeked inside, my mouth fell open.

Ethan was hunched over a wide table with headphones on. A worn blue t-shirt moved loosely over the muscles in his back as he used a hand tool to carve chunks out of a piece of grey material laid out in front of him.

After going over it a few times, he swept his hand across the table, causing a pile of curled grey shavings to fall to the floor.

It wasn't until I took my eyes off him, though, that I realized he was making prints. Tons of them by the looks of it. They covered every wall in the small, paint scented room.

I stepped inside to take them all in. There were cityscapes, abstract portraits of famous musicians, and multicolored animals that looked almost aboriginal with their bright colors and focused expressions. Others were obvious tributes to Van Gogh, Picasso, and Matisse.

It was such a wondrous surprise, and knowing the space was a secret made it even more overwhelming to behold.

After a while, I realized he must've been in some kind of trance or he would've noticed me in the doorway. "Ahem," I coughed, not wanting to startle him. "Ahem."

His head turned in my direction and he righted himself, yanking his earphones out at the same time.

I lifted my palms. "So this is what you've been hiding behind mystery door number one."

He looked as mortified as he did surprised, saying nothing as the blasting EDM poured from his headphones.

"Your dad mentioned once that you used to draw, but-"

He furrowed his brow. "He did?"

"Yeah." I walked over to him, unclipped the iPod from his sleeve, and turned it off. "But he said you stopped making art after your mom died."

He laid his iPod and headphones on the paint splattered wooden workbench behind him. "That's one version of events."

"What's the other?" I asked, mesmerized by the strange expression on his face.

"I'd say it's more accurate that my dad asked me to stop drawing after my mom died. So I started hiding it."

"And you're still hiding it?"

He swept some more linoleum shavings onto the floor. "No. I just don't advertise it."

"Well you should." I spun around, letting the medley of colors stream through my field of vision. "These are fabulous."

"Thanks."

"Why do you lock this room?" I asked, walking over to one of the walls.

He shrugged. "Because this is my private thing, and I don't want other people ruining it with their criticism and-"

I looked over my shoulder. "I suppose I should've knocked."

"It's always a mess in here, too, and locking the door is a lot easier than trying to keep it clean."

I laughed. "Like that closet my mom has with all the laundry baskets that are filled with whatever crap was on the kitchen table before the last dozen times she was expecting company."

"Andy Warhol used to do that," he said.

"Yeah, well, the contents of Andy's kitchen table were probably a lot more interesting than the shit my mom accumulates." I started looking through a rack of zebra prints. Each one was different colors and had a little number in the bottom corner. "Is this okay?" I asked. "I realize I'm being nosy but-"

"You might as well have a look around. You'll never shut up about it otherwise."

"True," I said, coming to a stack of prints that reflected the image of a little boy holding a toy boat. "And I don't mean to be bossy-"

He laughed.

"But I wouldn't shut up about it if I were you either." I glanced over my shoulder.

He was leaning against the table, watching me snoop.

"You have real talent."

"You think?"

"Absolutely," I said. But something struck me as odd. None of the prints were once offs. I mean, I knew that was the whole point of making prints- that the artist could make countless editions of one design. But why make multiples if you never wanted to show them to anybody. "I think people would pay for these."

"I don't know about that."

"You're underselling yourself, Ethan. This stuff is great." I moved to the next wooden rack and started flicking through the prints. First I came to a few that looked like Sophia Loren, followed by Bridget Bardot on the beach in Planet of the Apes.

And then I froze.

The next image looked so familiar.

It seemed naive to think it was me, but it reminded me of a picture I saw of myself a long time ago, a picture where I was wishing on a dandelion. I kept turning page after page and- just like all the others- there were tens of them in all different colors.

"Is this me?" I turned to look at him.

He clenched his jaw.

I slid one of the numbered pictures out and watched his face as I lifted it. "Well?"

"Yeah," he said. "It is."

My stomach dropped. The photo must've been taken ten years ago. I remember because it was from the same roll of film that had Brandi's fourteenth birthday party in it. "Where did you find this picture?"

He folded his arms. "I took it from a shoe box in the linen closet-"

I turned an ear towards him. "When?"

"The day before I left for boarding school."

I looked back at the image he'd made. He'd carved out my cheekbones and every corner of my face. Even my eyelashes were defined, along with the little white seeds on the flower.

"But you hated me then." I laid the print across the top of the stack I'd been looking through and let my arms fall to my sides. "You couldn't stand me."

He pursed his lips.

I shook my head. "You thought I was-"

"Beautiful," he said. "I thought you were beautiful."

I swallowed. "But you ignored me." I crossed my arms and hugged myself. "You barely even said two words to me the year before you left."

He shrugged. "What was there to say?"

"I don't know- something nice- anything to let me know you didn't hate me."

"I couldn't do that, Jenny."

My voice was shaky. "But all this time I thought- and you-"

"Come here."

FORTY TWO
- Ethan -

She looked so small in my studio, especially compared to how big my feelings for her were.

"Why didn't you tell me?" she asked, stepping up to me.

I cocked my head. "Tell you what? That I loved you? I couldn't."

Her open eyes swept across my face. "Why not?"

"Cause I didn't know that was what it was."

She pursed her lips.

"I thought I was sick. I thought that the ways I wanted you were wrong, that the best thing I could do was leave you alone."

She raised her eyebrows. "Just like you tried to leave art alone? Because it seems to me you're not as good at running from your problems as you pretend to be."

Half my mouth curled up into a smile. "No shit."

Her eyes formed little crescents.

"Neither of you will leave me alone."

She raised a hand to my cheek. "I won't anyway."

I grabbed her hand and moved it against my chest.

"And I think the only way you're ever going to make peace with your art is to show it to someone," she said. "Because this is too big a talent for anyone to hide away."

"I'd like to," I said, stepping back to sit down on one side of the workbench.

She sat on the other.

"But it's not to everyone's taste." My dad's anger at my doodling was still so fresh in my mind. How the hell would he feel if he knew I'd graduated to paints, that I had the audacity to number my prints? "And it's all so personal. I can't bear the thought of it being rejected."

She shook her head. "You don't get it. That's how you know you're making something worthwhile. Because not everyone gets it. That's the whole point of art- to force people to have an opinion, to force them to think, to feel."

I found her conviction refreshing.

"I had a drama teacher once who said you haven't made it until you have critics."

I nodded. "I suppose that makes sense."

"But getting critics isn't the point. It's all about that One Fan. That one person who finds your work soothing or entertaining or amusing or meaningful-"

I narrowed my eyes at her.

"And that's who you do it for. That's why you take the risk of letting people see it. Because one person might like it, and that's how you know you did the right thing not keeping it to yourself."

"I appreciate your optimism," I said. "But what if that one person never comes along."

She smiled. "You don't have to worry about that."

I raised my eyebrows.

"She already has."

I felt my breath catch in my throat.

"I mean it, Ethan. This stuff is incredible. I feel so grateful that I've seen it, and I know others would feel the same."

I ran a hand over my head.

"Besides-" She laid a hand on my knee. "Isn't it what your mom would've wanted?"

I took a deep breath and looked around. Was she right? Was it pointless to keep my creations to myself if someone else would benefit? After all, isn't that what I always wanted? For someone to say, "Hey- your stuff isn't crap."

It certainly felt good to hear Jenny say it now, especially since she was the person whose validation meant the most.

"It's only a suggestion," she said. "You don't have to decide today."

"That's a relief," I said. "Because to be honest, I have enough to worry about right now."

She squinted at me. "Like what?"

"Like the fact that I want you so bad I feel sick. Just like I did when I was seventeen."

She stood up, reached for my linoleum cutter, and handed it to me. Then she picked up the sheet I'd been working on and slid it onto my drying rack. "May I?" she asked, pointing to a stack of untouched lino in the corner.

I nodded.

She laid a fresh sheet down and walked to the end of my workbench. Then she pulled her shirt off over her head.

I gripped the smooth handle of the cutter in my hand as she unhooked her bra.

She dropped it on the floor with her shirt.

I felt my pulse bounce in my throat.

Next, she unzipped her jeans and pulled them down, taking her underwear with them.

I wanted to ask what the hell she was doing, but I didn't dare interrupt.

She sat down on the edge of my workbench with her back towards me.

My eyes traveled along the curve of her hip to her waist and up her spine. Her skin was so smooth, so perfect. If it weren't for a cluster of freckles on one shoulder, I might've thought she was made of marble.

"Okay," she said, looking over her shoulder. "Let's see how you do when you have permission to use me as a muse."

I scooted towards her on the bench and took a deep breath.

She ran her hand through her hair and shook it out behind her.

I laid a hand on her hip and slid it towards her waist, studying the angle of the perfect slope.

"Art first," she said. "Nookie later."

"I'm just trying to get a grip on your dimensions," I whispered, sneaking a hand around to cup one of her breasts.

She slapped it away. "They're not going to be in the picture."

"Oops. My bad." I smiled and slid my hand down her stomach, hoping to reach between her legs.

She crossed them. "What did I just say, you rascal?"

"I don't know if I can make art when I'm-"

She looked over her shoulder and raised her eyebrows. "When you're what?"

"About to tear through my pants."

"Try," she said, her eyes pleading. "For me."

I sighed. Then I stood and stepped up to the table, angling the grey sheet towards her. For a moment, I just admired the way the summer sunshine peaked through the blinds and highlighted the subtle curves of her back.

But as my dick strained in my pants, it was easy to understand why doing this never occurred to me before. And yet I didn't want to let her down, especially since she was right.

I had used her as a muse without her permission- more times than she would ever know. The least I could do was restrain myself long enough to get the shape of her back right along with the flicks at the ends of her hair.

And as she materialized on the page, my desire for her only grew.

"How's it going?" she asked after a few minutes of silence.

"Honestly?" I wove the cutter through the linoleum, keeping my eyes on her. "I think this might be my masterpiece."

FORTY THREE
- Jenny -

I was thrilled to have his eyes on my body.

I could almost feel his intense focus burning my skin, while the only sounds I could hear were my shallow breathing and the occasional sweep of his hand as he knocked the grey shavings to the floor.

I couldn't wait to see what he'd done. To have him sculpt my curves in the grey block was almost as exciting as having his hands on me, and as he worked, my anticipation grew.

Of course, the longer I sat under his gaze, the keener I became to reward his efforts.

"You know this is just the block I'll use to make the prints, right?" he asked. "It's not done after this."

"For today it is," I said, flicking my eyes up at him.

A subtle smile crossed his face, and a spark caught fire in my core.

"I think it would be better if your tits were in it."

"Too bad," I said. "I'm the client, and this is how I want it."

He raised his eyebrows. "The client? I didn't realize I was going to get paid."

"Handsomely," I said, my eyes flashing at him again.

"Don't torture me, Jen. I can barely keep my hand steady as it is."

"Let me know when it gets really bad," I said. "I'll let you pull my hair to steady it."

He clenched his jaw and looked back down at the sheet.

Perhaps he thought I was kidding, but I wasn't. Being his muse was my first official role in this city, and I was loving every second of it. To be honest, I don't think I would've felt any luckier if I was Nico herself, stumbling into a Velvet Underground jam session.

And my desire for him was not only becoming unmanageable, but it was making me feel uncharacteristically bold.

I mean, wanting him in vain was one thing, but now that I'd had him all to myself and deep inside me, I knew there was only one thing that could relieve my insatiable craving.

What's more, I was eager to prove to him that I wanted him as bad as he wanted me, that I wanted him more than all the women he'd had combined, and that he didn't have to be gentle with me.

After all, I didn't want to be pigeonholed as his high school wannabe sweetheart. I wanted to be the star of his darker fantasies, too- the ones it would make him blush to tell me about.

Because I knew I'd do anything to be his everything.

And watching him watch me was all the foreplay I needed.

"How's it coming along?" I asked.

"I'm almost done," he said. "You can see it in a second."

I was so excited I was on the edge of my seat. No one had ever drawn or painted me before- besides him, of course- and I felt like I had my own private artist.

"Are we there yet?" I asked.

"Patience is a virtue," he said, throwing a sliver of linoleum at me.

I rolled my eyes.

"Okay," he said, bending down and blowing the shavings away. "The linocut for my first ever commissioned piece is done."

I smiled and stood to face him.

His eyes dripped down my naked body as slowly as liquid soap.

I pretended not to notice.

"Well, well, well," I said, stepping between him and what he'd carved. "So you carved away the bits that you don't want to take the paint, right?"

"Exactly."

I turned around and looked up at him. "As far as I can tell, it's coming along quite nicely."

He smiled.

I laid the palm of my hand over the bulge in his pants. "Along with your other works in progress."

He clenched his jaw.

I stuck my hands under his soft t-shirt and pulled it off over his head so his solid chest was only a few inches from mine.

Then I took the linoleum cutter from his hand. It had a smooth, wooden handle and a short metal tip. I held it backwards and laid it against his chest. "And is this how you got so chiseled?" I asked, dragging it along the lines of his stomach.

He kept his eyes on me, his abs flexing with his breath.

I reached behind me and laid the tool on the table.

Then I undid one button of his jeans at a time until the heat in his pants was bursting against the back of my fingers.

He raised his eyebrows. "Ready for me again so soon?"

I stood on my tip toes to whisper in his ear. "Gagging for it."

He exhaled and stood still as I kept undressing him, first by sticking my hands down the sides of his pants and then by forcing them down over his ass.

His cock sprang up between us, and I stepped forward so it was pressed against my stomach.

"Your turn to have a seat," I said, nodding at the bench behind him.

He stepped backwards out of his pants and looked over his shoulder to find his way. By the time he sat down and looked up, I was standing between his knees.

He put one hand on my waist and slipped the other between my legs. "You know I can't get enough of you."

I put my hands on his broad shoulders and inhaled as he slid his fingertips along my slit. "Promise me you won't stop trying," I said, squeezing my hands around his shoulders.

I moaned as he slipped his fingers inside me, sending waves of warmth straight through me like rising bubbles. "Oh god, Ethan." It was incredible to think his name had been a whisper on my lips for so long and that now, after all this time, he could hear me aching for him.

He churned his fingers inside me and took one of my breasts in his warm mouth.

I felt like an instrument in his capable hands, an instrument that was being played for the first time.

And it felt so good to give myself to him, to be wanted like that, to know I'd been wanted like that for so long. It was the best feeling in the world.

And it was time to return the favor.

I put my hands around his face and pulled his mouth from my pursed nipple.

"What?" he asked, his thick eyebrows furrowing.

I bent over and kissed his mouth, relishing the taste of the lips that had been a forbidden fruit for so long.

Then I sank to my knees and laid my hand against his cock, the same cock that had deflowered me the night before.

"I want to taste you," I whispered, glancing up at him as I curled my fingers around his shaft.

He slid a hand into my hair and pulled it back to get a better look at my face. "I thought you'd never ask."

FORTY FOUR
- Ethan -

The most incredible woman I knew was kneeling before me with my dick in her hands.

I didn't know what I did to deserve it, but I was thanking my lucky fucking stars.

"Don't be afraid to tell me how you like it," she said, her breasts squeezed together as she started stroking my shaft. "I want this to be good for you."

The pressure in my dick was so intense I couldn't even smile.

But I knew it was going to be good. Because I didn't just want this goddess in front me, I fucking worshipped her. So the fact that she was looking up at me from between my legs was such a rush I wasn't sure which of my heads was going to explode first.

When she parted her lips, I wrapped my hands around the back of the wooden bench and clenched my jaw as she flicked her tongue around the tip of my dick, my stomach tightening between us.

By the time she flattened her tongue and started licking me, I was so hot for her it was hard not to thrust myself between her fat lips.

Thank god she finally wrapped her mouth around me before I passed out from the suspense.

I don't know why it was so intense. I'd had more blow jobs than I could recall, but this was different. Not only was Jen incredibly sexy, but her enthusiasm in pleasuring me was so fucking hot I couldn't do anything but watch as she slid her lips up and down my swollen shaft, squeezing me in her hands.

And if I thought I was conflicted about my feelings for her before, this event threw me into a whole new level of confusion because while I wanted it to last forever, I also wanted her to suck me faster.

After all, I knew better than to think I could last with this dream come true on the end of my dick.

I reached for the back of her head and rested my hand on it.

She sped up without any pushing.

I groaned.

She groaned.

Tingles shot up my spine, and I felt my balls swell. "Fuck, Jenny."

She sped up again, her hand and mouth moving in tandem.

It was too much.

"I'm gonna come," I said, swelling between her lips. I didn't want to take her by surprise so I repeated it, but she only tightened her grip and sucked me harder.

I took my hand from her head and gripped the bench so hard I expected I'd have splinters by the time she was done. Then I exhaled and let my head fall back.

My body jerked a second later.

I felt my hot seed spill into her throat, relieving the pressure I'd felt in my temples.

When I dropped my head, she was swallowing me in big greedy gulps, drinking me down like she'd been looking forward to it all day.

A growl rumbled up my throat as I watched her.

Not even a drop escaped her lips as she milked me right down her throat, her eyelashes casting long shadows on her cheeks.

It was only then that I realized I was out of breath.

She released my dick and wiped her mouth on the back of her fingers, a self-conscious blush sweeping across her cheeks as she looked up at me.

"That was incredible," I said, pushing a wisp of hair from her face.

"Yeah?"

"Yeah." I cocked my head. "I mean, with a little practice-"

She smiled and rolled her eyes.

I reached down to help her up.

She rose to her feet and reached out for one of my shoulders.

I put my hands on her hips and spun her around, smoothing one hand over her ass.

She looked over her shoulder. "Penny for your thoughts?"

I smiled. "You can have 'em for free." I stood up and walked her forward until the front of her thighs were pressed against my worktable and my dick was pressed against her ass.

Then I buried my face in her hair and lifted one of her knees up onto the table.

She leaned forward and planted her hands on the lino block so they were halfway up the image of her I'd carved.

Then I reached down, grabbed my cock, and forced her open.

She gasped as I thrust inside her until the firm cheeks of her ass sank down to the base of my wet shaft.

Then I reached around and rubbed her clit, crushing it against my dick to show her how hard I still was for her.

"Oh god," she breathed. She righted herself and reached behind her, wrapping her arms around my neck.

I squeezed one of her tits in my hand, pinching her nipple too hard between my fingers. "You like that?" I whispered, working her hot clit like crazy. "You gonna coat my dick?"

She moaned and arched her back, forcing her head against my chest. "Oh, Ethan."

My name on her lips energized me. I put my hands on her waist and began pounding my hips against her ass.

She fell forwards onto the table, her breasts bouncing above the lino image as my balls smacked against her.

She cried out but didn't tell me to stop so I fucked her deep like I knew she'd never had it, digging my fingers into her flesh.

When her breathing became a series of gasps, I reached around her bent leg and flicked her bud again, working it in circles as I slowed my pace, massaging her at the spot where I'd forced her open.

"Yeah," she panted. "Right there."

I bent over her, rocking her deep until her bud burned my fingertips. "Come for me, Jenny."

She whimpered and turned her head at the moment her lips fell apart. Then she cried out, her body jerking in my hands as she throbbed around my dick.

I squeezed my eyes shut and savored the feeling of her pouring down on me as her tight pussy choked the base of my shaft.

The top half of her body collapsed against the table.

I leaned upright and admired the way the arch in her back curved up to her raised ass. Then I thrust inside her gently, riding out her orgasm as I smoothed my hand over her pale cheek.

Fuck she was beautiful.

And I wasn't just in deep literally. I was hopelessly head over fucking heels for her, too.

And I didn't want to feel sick about it anymore.

I wanted to feel good about it.

Like I did in that moment.

And I wanted her to feel good about her feelings for me, too.

Because didn't we deserve a little bit of bliss in this fucked up world?

Besides, Jenny was right.

Beautiful things shouldn't be hidden away.

FLASHBACK
- Ethan -

The day they got married we had to take a family photo…

Jenny wore a light blue dress that she spent the whole day fidgeting with. Every time I looked at her she was either yanking it up or yanking it down.

Meanwhile, I was at that age where I was not only expected to dance with all the little girls, but anyone over sixty still thought it was acceptable to squeeze my cheeks.

And every time I felt miserable, I would look around for Jenny.

I took comfort in the fact that she looked similarly dejected.

Of course, I knew better than to take it personally. If anything, I figured she must have realized how controlling my dad was. What's more, the way her mom looked at him sickened me. I couldn't imagine how she must have felt.

I decided I should say something.

I just didn't know what.

At one point, I found her sitting at a round table in the corner of the room. She was busy mashing a piece of wedding cake into its icing to make a thick paste.

I sat a few chairs away from her and watched her sculpt it upwards with two forks, not really making anything but a mess.

"You gonna eat that?" I asked.

I meant it as a joke, but she didn't laugh. Instead, she just glanced at me out of the corner of her eye before carrying on.

I finished two half-drunk glasses of wine that were within reach and made my way outside the tent to see if I could get in on a game of bags.

Back to the photo…

Neither of us is smiling with our eyes in it, which is especially apparent because our parents look ridiculously pleased with themselves.

But what you can't see in the portrait is that I'm holding Jenny's hand.

I only reached for it at the last second- partly so she would stop fidgeting with her dress and partly because I felt the urge to.

I still remember how my chest felt when she wrapped her fingers around mine. It was just for a brief moment, just long enough to let me know she hadn't brushed my hand by accident or regretted taking it.

And in a split second, it turned the worst day ever into one of the best.

But as much her touch helped to relieve the pain I felt that day, I knew by the time the camera flashed that holding her hand would never be enough.

FORTY FIVE
- Jenny -

I felt like I couldn't love who I wanted for so long.

It was like being in the closet.

But now I was finally out. At least to myself.

And it was a liberating experience, one that made me feel lighter than I ever had.

And hornier, too, but Brandi always warned me that would be that case.

I mean, on the few occasions I could ever recall her having a dry spell, she would inevitably settle into it and become increasingly happy to avoid the single's scene.

But as soon as she got a man on her radar, she was like a cat who'd just tried real meat for the first time, and she'd be all, like, "fuck another Whiskas dry food movie night with you, this pussy wants steak."

Her words, not mine.

Anyway, I finally understood what she was on about because the more I slept with Ethan, and the more time we spent together, the more the thought of us being apart made me shudder.

Unfortunately, after about two weeks, I started getting sick of keeping my perfect boyfriend a secret.

After all, as long as we kept our feelings between us, we were still sort of swimming against the current, whereas I was ready to relax into our metaphorical relationship inner tube and see what was around the river bend.

In other words, I was so head over heels I was constantly making ridiculous analogies to try and explain my smitten status, and I'd never felt gayer in my life.

It was like living in a fucking musical where every scene was more wonderful than the last… there I go again.

Anyway, one afternoon when I was particularly high on love, I turned my key in the apartment door and pushed it open.

The door to Ethan's studio was ajar- as it often was now that he'd let me in on his little hobby. But when I peeked in, he wasn't inside.

My jaw still dropped, though.

I took a few steps towards the easel where the print of my naked back was propped up. He'd made it bright red with yellow accents, and it was striking.

And as I approached it, I noticed there were more on the drying rack at the side of the room that he'd made using a variety of other bright colors.

My chest swelled with pride as I heard the apartment door swing open and shut behind me.

He walked in wiping his hands on his favorite pair of paint splattered jeans. "Jenny."

"I love them."

He smiled. "Yeah?"

I nodded.

"I like them, too," he said. "But you should see the model. They really don't do her justice."

I couldn't suppress my wide smile. "She must be really beautiful then."

"Blindingly," he said, tucking a strand of hair behind my ear.

I hooked my fingers in the loops of his jeans. "How will I ever compete with her for your attention?"

"I have a few ideas," he said, a mischievous grin giving his filthy thoughts away.

I smacked his chest.

"How was your audition?"

"It was okay."

He furrowed his brow. "Just okay?"

I shrugged. "I got the sense that the director already made his mind up and was only sitting through the auditions because people bothered showing up."

He cocked his head.

"Either that or he's a robot who only stays alive by playing games on his phone."

He scrunched his face. "Sorry."

"It's okay," I said. "I'm actually feeling more optimistic with every audition."

"Each no gets you closer to a yes."

"That's what I'm telling myself. Plus, Ira has kept his promise of getting me seen."

"I suppose that's true."

I ran a finger down his chest. "I hope you thanked your friend for me- Ira's nephew who got me the appointment in the first place?"

"Why don't you thank him yourself?"

I raised my eyebrows.

"I want you to come to the club tomorrow."

"Are you sure you'll be able to concentrate if I'm there?"

"Actually, it's for a private party so I'll be slacking off pretty hard."

"I would like to see where you work."

"And I'd like you to meet my friends."

"Really?"

He nodded and pulled me towards him.

"Would I be meeting them as your stepsister or-"

"You'll be meeting them as my wet hot lover."

I laughed and looked down to hide my burning cheeks.

"What do you say?"

I looked up at him and furrowed my brow. "Are you sure?"

"Of course I'm sure."

"What's the party for?"

"It's an engagement party," he said. "For my boss."

"Ben?"

He nodded. "One of many if I had to guess."

"And you want me to be your date?"

"Date, drinking buddy- whatever you want to call it."

"And what if someone asks how we met?"

He squinted at the ceiling before looking back at me. "Say I saved you from a burning building."

I rolled my eyes.

"I would you know."

"Yeah, but-"

"Or that I pulled you out of the Hudson after your tour boat capsized."

I squinted at him.

"Or that I threw myself in front of a bus to keep you from getting-"

"Why does it have to be a story about you saving me?" I folded my arms. "Why don't we tell them that I saved you?"

"We could," he said. "But lying is more fun."

I fixed my eyes on him. "Oh, that's the truth, then, is it? That I saved you?"

"More times than you know."

I pursed my lips.

"To be honest, I don't care what you tell them, and I care even less what they think."

I took a deep breath, my inhale forcing my chest towards his.

"All I care about is giving my friends a chance to meet the reason I'm in such a good mood these days."

"You are in a pretty good mood."

He laughed. "I know. I'm almost so smug I'm annoying myself."

"Well, in that case, I'd be delighted to introduce myself as the reason you've gotten so annoying."

"Great, because I already said you'd come."

I craned my neck forwards. "You did?!"

"Yeah," he said, backing out of the room. "I figured once you knew I'd be there, you wouldn't be able to resist coming along."

I shook my head and followed after him.

He opened the fridge and pulled out a bottle of water.

"Only if you're sure," I said, sliding onto one of the barstools.

"Why the doubts?" he asked, leaning a hand on the counter. "Why wouldn't I be sure?"

"I don't know." I shrugged. "I guess because once I meet your friends, you can't take it back."

"Take what back?"

"This," I said, waving my hands between us. "Along with everything that's happened between these walls in the last two weeks."

"Why would I want to take any of this back? It would be like returning the only gift I ever really wanted."

I reached for his water. "Is that what this feels like to you?"

He handed me the bottle. "Of course. I've wanted you since I got on the bus that day-"

"And completely ignored me."

"What can I say? It was part of my slow seduction strategy."

I laughed and set the bottle on the counter. "It was slow alright. I nearly died waiting."

He raised his finger. "It was worth the wait in the end, though."

"Was it?" I asked, cocking my head. "I can't really remember. It's been so long since I saw any of your moves-"

And with that, he scooped me off the barstool and fireman carried me to the bedroom.

FORTY SIX
- Ethan -

I could tell she was nervous on the way to the club.

She kept making me check her teeth for lip gloss, and she was fidgeting like crazy, pushing her hair in front of her ear and then behind it and then in front of it and then-

"You look great, Jen."

She looked at me through grateful eyes. "Sorry. I'm a little nervous."

"I know," I said, clocking a passing street sign. "But there's no reason to be. My friends are going to love you."

"And if they don't?"

"Then they aren't my fucking friends anymore, how's that?"

She scrunched her face. "Excessive?"

"Look, it's an engagement party for two people who are in the mood to celebrate happy couples, and seeing as how we just became one, we'll fit right in."

"Did we become one?" she asked, cocking her head. "When did that happen?"

"Around the time I made that print and you dropped to your-"

She elbowed me in the ribs and glanced in the rearview mirror, but our Uber driver didn't seem to be paying attention. "Speaking of inappropriate," she said. "When I first met Ira, he said he expected me to be more butch."

I raised my eyebrows.

"And bald. He thought I was going to be bald."

I swallowed.

"Is anyone at this party expecting me to be bald and butch?" She turned an ear towards me. "Because I'd really like to know now if I'm going to disappoint."

I sighed.

"Well?"

"Christophe will probably be surprised."

"And why is that?"

"Because when you first came to town, he started asking all these questions about you, and I wanted to squash his interest."

"By telling him I was a hairless lesbian?"

"By encouraging him to stop trying to picture you naked."

"Sounds like a real charmer."

"Oh he is," I said.

"Anything else I should know?"

I squinted at her. "You probably shouldn't tell everyone how in love with me you are."

She blinked.

"Because I don't want our love to overshadow the happy couple's."

"You're so full of it."

I reached around and squeezed her waist. "You're going to be so full of it if you don't watch it."

She smiled. "I better be."

"It has been a full two hours since-"

"I just hope we can make it to the end of the party."

"If there's an emergency, just say the code word."

She furrowed her brows. "What's the code word?"

I glanced at the driver and put a finger over my lips.

"How am I supposed to say the code word if I don't know what it is-"

"I'll know."

"And what if you don't pick up on it?"

"I will."

She narrowed her eyes at me.

"And if I don't for some reason, just drink your whole drink all at once."

She raised her eyebrows. "That's a signal you won't miss, is it?"

"It's a signal I'm highly trained to notice."

She groaned and looked out her window but crossed her bare legs towards me.

It felt great to have her as my date, but she was so much more than that.

In the last two weeks, we'd sunk into a domestic routine that I was already getting used to… apart from how regularly I was waking up in the night with a dead arm from holding her while we slept.

But that was the kind of thing we could get better at in time.

And I was willing to work at it.

That's how I knew it was serious.

I'd met lots of women in the past that I had chemistry with, women who were great in bed and good company and easy on the eyes. But none of them were perfect.

And neither was Jen. But in her case, I was willing to put up with the occasional disagreement, the occasional clogged sink, and the occasional wet towel on the bed.

If anything, I felt kind of lucky to be the guy with her hair in my sink, the guy who knew all her little quirks.

I knew what Taylor Swift songs she liked to sing in the shower, knew the weird way she ate Kit Kats so the wafer was the last part to go. I even knew when she was tired because she'd get so visibly cold her lips would change color.

And with every little oddity I learned about, I fell for her a little more.

I was especially enamored of the way she bit her lip before she dropped down to give me head, which she'd done only two hours ago in the shower.

Hence my being so relaxed.

But it wasn't just the sex. She was everything I could ever want in a woman- everything I ever had wanted- and it made the whole thing pretty surreal.

"I guess there's a lot riding on tonight," she said, looking back my way.

I furrowed my brow. "Why do you say that?"

"Because." She shrugged. "If this goes well we might think about telling our parents."

I clenched my jaw.

"Unless you think this is a short term-"

"Of course I don't," I said, putting a hand on her knee.

"So why the long face?"

"There's a chance they won't understand."

"A very good chance," she said. "But don't you think they would in time?"

"I like to think so."

"That's why I think the sooner we come clean, the sooner we can relax."

"I feel pretty relaxed as it is."

"Well, I don't," she said. "I hate feeling like I have to hide how happy I am from the people I care about."

"I'm glad you're happy."

She sighed. "Too happy maybe."

"Why too happy?"

"Because I'm on such an ecstatic level of happiness it feels unsustainable."

"Me too," I said. "But no matter what happens, we'll get through it."

She smiled and leaned her head on my shoulder. "I suppose we've survived being miserable together before, too."

"Yeah, but we'll never be that unhappy again."

"How do you know?"

"Because I'm never going to let anything come between us again, least of all anyone else's agenda."

She lifted her head. "That means a lot coming from the best roommate I ever had."

I rolled my eyes. "I can't tell if that's a promotion or a demotion."

"It just is what it is. That's all. No labels necessary."

"I suppose labels have caused us some heartache in the past."

She nodded. "Too much."

"So how will we explain it to my old man?"

She shrugged. "I don't know yet, but it's not going to be with the leaked sex tape idea you suggested last night."

I smiled. "Shouldn't we make one just in case?"

"Only if I can't get a break without it."

My face dropped. "You wouldn't really consider-"

"Shame on you," she said, smacking my chest. "As if."

FORTY SEVEN
- Jenny -

He was a complete gentleman. Not only did he introduce me to everyone perfectly- as Jenny- but his hand was constantly finding my lower back just when I needed it to.

Most of the guests were concentrated in a large VIP room at the back of the club.

Apparently the bride to be, Carrie, decorated it herself, which is how she met Ben. There were quite a few toasts that made jokes about it. I guess she moved on to his apartment once he put a ring on it- a gorgeous ring at that.

After Ethan introduced me to his friends, we got some drinks and took a seat at one of the scalloped tables jutting out from the wall.

"There are some other people I have to say hi to," he said. "But they aren't important."

"Does that mean I've embarrassed you already?" I looked down at an invisible watch. "We haven't even been here for two hours."

"I'm genuinely trying to spare you, but you're welcome to come if you want."

A pretty brunette with two much eye makeup appeared beside the table in a black dress that I believe was supposed to look deliberately disheveled. "How about all these rich people, huh?"

Ethan smiled. "Nora, this is Jenny."

She raised her eyebrows. "Your Jenny, I take it?"

"My Jenny," he said, squeezing my knee under the table.

"In that case, I'll spare her the stories you're least proud," she said, sitting down.

I reached across the table and shook her hand.

"Can I get you a drink?" Ethan asked, raising his eyebrows.

"Only if you can get it faster than Woody can."

Ethan stood up. "Glad to know he's already on the case."

I tried to give Ethan a look that said, "Who is this person and why are you leaving me with her?"

"You'll be happier here with Nora," he said. "I promise. And I would've introduced you to Woody already if I'd seen him but-"

"We just got here," Nora said, batting her caked eyelashes.

Ethan pointed at her. "No stories."

She rolled her eyes.

I watched him walk away.

"Might want to tuck your tongue back in your mouth," she said.

"Sorry." I scrunched my face. "This is just still kind of new."

"You don't have to explain." She leaned back in the tall booth. "I get it."

Could she possibly?

"You know all those Tinder horror stories you read about online?" she asked.

I nodded.

"They're all mine."

"What?"

"All of them," she said. "Or the equivalent."

"I see."

"And then last year I met- get this- a homeless guy, well, formerly homeless, and I'm in deeper, cheesier love than I ever thought a weirdo like me deserved."

"I know the feeling."

She cocked her head. "Cause you're a weirdo, too?"

I shrugged.

She nodded. "I can tell."

I raised my eyebrows.

"I bet if Ethan met you ten years ago, you guys never would've worked."

What the fuck?

"I mean, he's such a jock, and you're obviously like a drama geek or something."

I squinted at her. "What makes you say that?"

"You just have that extra flair about you that other people don't have."

"Is that so?"

She nodded. "I mean, I only picked up on it because my best friend works in a gallery."

"Oh yeah?"

"So I'm sensitive to creative types."

"Wow."

"I'm right, aren't I?" she asked.

I nodded. "You are."

"Like, you seem kind of shy, but I bet if someone pumped you full of vodka and handed you the mic, you'd be doing lines from the Tempest in no time."

I laughed. "You're nuts."

"So is my boyfriend. He's the same. Totally reserved unless he's sure he's got your full attention, in which case you better be in the mood for a dramatic monologue."

"Is he an actor, too?"

"No, a poet. He also does security here."

I furrowed my brow. "And what about you?"

"I'm Carrie's assistant."

"So you saw all the love blossom between her and Ben?"

She nodded. "Front row seats."

"That must've been nice."

"Meh." She shrugged. "It's better when it's happening to you."

"Agreed."

"You been in love before?" she asked, eyeing my drink.

"Do you want some?" I slid it towards her. "To hold you over until your knight arrives with yours?"

"Thanks." She took a healthy swig and scooted it back towards me. "Ooh that's nice. I wish I'd asked for that."

"It's some kind of boozy Shirley Temple, I guess."

She smiled, her plum lips bringing out her bright teeth. "Sounds dangerous."

"Time will tell," I said, reaching for my straw.

"So is this your first time?"

"At Club Abbott or-"

"No, being in love."

"Yeah." My first for a long time, more like.

"Think it's your last?"

I smiled. "I hope so."

"You guys are cute together."

"Thanks."

"And Ethan's amazing."

"I know."

She leaned forward. "I was only teasing him about the stories before," she said. "Most of the ones I know about only make him look good."

"Oh?"

"One night I was here, and he gave a girl mouth to mouth and literally saved her life."

"He never mentioned that."

"It was really scary and awesome."

"Sounds like it."

"Always nice to have a boyfriend who gives good mouth to mouth, anyway."

My cheeks burned.

"There was another night when some guy fell while he was dancing and opened his hand up on his busted beer bottle."

I raised my eyebrows.

"And his hand was literally spurting blood like he was straight out of some crappy horror flick."

"Oh my god."

"And Ethan picked out the glass and, like, tied up his arm so he wouldn't bleed out before the ambulance got here."

I knew without asking where he tied it. His dad made me do drills for hand wounds every weekend the summer before I went to school.

"Hmmm," she said, her eyes rolling up to the ceiling. "What else?"

"I guess he took a lot of girls home before I came along?"

"Yeah, but based on the eyes you made at him when he walked away, it doesn't look like you've been disappointed by his experience."

"So what you're telling me is that he's a total hero and doesn't have any skeletons in the closet."...Besides his feelings for me.

"Pretty much."

"Did he slip you some money to say that nice stuff?"

She shook her head. "No. But if you tell him I made him look good, he'll probably plow me with free drinks next time I'm in."

"In that case, I'll be sure to make a fuss."

"Do," she said. "You'll have to come in with me, too. We'll get fall down. It'll be fab."

"Sounds like fun."

"Can't do it tonight, though, unfortunately. Not with all the Who's Who milling about. But maybe next weekend if you're around?"

"Sure."

"Will you be around for a while or…?"

I nodded. "Hopefully. I mean, ideally I'll get a part in something soon so I can at least afford to stay out here a little longer and keep chasing my big break."

"Oh cool. Well, if you need someone to show you all the best cheap places to eat and where you can get away with drinking in public, I'm your girl."

I smiled.

"And I might be going out on a limb here, but if you like going to weird artsy fartsy stuff- and you don't want to ruin your solid relationship by forcing Ethan to go along- my boyfriend and I will go to just about anything as long as the tickets are cheap."

"I will definitely take you up on that," I said. "And I'm sure that offer is good for at least a few extra free drinks from Ethan."

She smiled. "Excellent."

"Now, before I forget," I said, leaning forward and scooting my drink her way. "Tell me more about your friend's gallery."

FORTY EIGHT
- Ethan -

She was amazing.

And smart, funny, elegant, charming… No one ever would've guessed that she was from a small town where the most important events happened outside the local Dairy Queen.

And every time my eyes came to rest on her across the room, I felt my chest swell. Once, I even looked down expecting to see beams of light.

She got along with everyone. I wasn't really worried that she wouldn't, but I'd taken women out who weren't secure enough in themselves to be around people who had so much going for them.

But it was no sweat for Jenny, and frankly, having her on my arm made me feel as lucky and rich as everyone else in the room.

I looked across the elevator at her shiny eyes. She'd been the life of the party when we'd walked out, but she crashed pretty hard about halfway home- probably as a result of trying to keep up with Nora all night.

Her hair was a mess from laying on my shoulder in the cab and her shoes dangled from her fingertips.

"You were amazing tonight," I said as the elevator came to a stop on my floor.

"I felt it," she said, taking my arm. "Though it would be hard not to around all those people."

"I'm glad you liked them."

"I really did." She leaned against the wall outside my door. "Everyone was so nice. And I think Nora and I could really be friends."

"From where I was standing, it looks like you already are."

"She and Woody are ridiculously cute together."

I nodded. "That guy is an inspiration."

"Totally." She smiled. "And I can see why you like Ben so much. He's so charming and-"

I scoffed. "Yeah. To be honest, if he weren't engaged, I never would've introduced him to you." I pushed the door open for her.

She walked in, flicking on the kitchen light and dropping her shoes at the same time. "Why not?"

"Because I like being the charmer in your life," I said, leaning against the door to close it.

"You are," she said, her heavy lashes batting as she stepped up to me. "And if I still want you after meeting all those incredible people, you must be quite a catch."

I slung my hands around her lower back, and she let the weight of her lithe body lean on me.

Her face was full of concentration as she dragged a finger along my bottom lip. "Unrequited love is so overrated, eh?" she asked, raising her eyes to mine.

"I'm glad you had a good time," I said. "I was so proud to have you there with me."

She squinted.

"What?"

"You wouldn't have been proud to be with me ten years ago."

"Ten years ago I wasn't secure enough to be with someone so dazzling."

She rolled her eyes.

"Not to mention our family arrangement."

"Speaking of dazzling, I have some news."

I raised my eyebrows.

"It's a surprise." She pushed herself upright against my chest and went to the cupboard for a glass. "Hopefully a good one."

"I'm listening," I said, leaning against the counter.

She filled her glass at the sink.

"Is it a surprise like the one I got in the shower before the party?"

She smiled, her eyes smaller than usual from so many drinks. "I can't guarantee you'll be quite that excited about it, but-"

"Spit it out already."

She turned towards me and leaned a hip against the counter. "I found a gallery where you can have your first exhibition."

"What?"

"Nora's bestie works in a gallery that showcases local, undiscovered talent every week."

I swallowed.

"And she's going to send me the info so we can get you in."

"I don't know."

She raised her hand to the studio room behind me. "You can't just hoard all that precious art."

"You're the only one who thinks it's precious."

She set her glass down. "Because I'm the only one you've shown it to."

"Can I think about it?"

She shook her head. "No. That's your whole problem. You thinking about it. You're supposed to enjoy making it and let other people think about it. Let other people figure out what it means to them."

I stepped up and drained the rest of her glass of water.

"Say yes," she said. "They might not even accept you, but you have to try. You can't just be the sole owner all your limited edition prints. It's a waste of your talent."

I sighed. "Kind of like if you were to give up all your ambition to stay home and make X-rated movies with me."

She pressed a finger against my chest. "Exactly. Excellent analogy."

I groaned.

"Say yes."

"Let me ask you something," I said.

"Shoot."

"Are you ever going to let this go?"

She shook her head, her eyes full of drunken defiance.

I smiled. "In that case, I'm willing to negotiate-"

"No negotiations. Just promise you'll send in a portfolio of your work, and if they won't take it then-"

"You didn't even let me finish."

She sighed. "Fine. Tell me about your conditions you stubborn artist you."

I laughed.

"I'll do it," I said. "If you'll move in with me."

She furrowed her brows. "I already have."

"No. You showed up, and I looked the other way-"

"You looked right down my shirt is what you did."

"Jenny."

"What?"

"Listen for a second."

"Fine," she said. "But you should know it feels kind of awkward when you throw it in my face that I showed up uninvited-"

"Shut up."

She swallowed.

"I want you to stay officially. I want to drive across the country and pick up your shoes and crap so you're not living out of a suitcase. I want to get you a robe of your own so you never feel like you have to get dressed. I want to throw half of my clothes away to make room for your stuff, and I want you to be my mine for good. No secrets. No doubts. No unrequited bullshit ever again."

Half her mouth curled into a smile. "Just tons and tons of requiting?"

I nodded. "Yeah. You and me. Together at last. No more wasting time apart."

She squinted at me. "You're not worried this is all happening a bit fast?"

"No," I said, looking down at the freckles on her nose. "If anything, it's all happened way too fucking slow, and I feel this horrible pressure in my chest to make up for lost time."

"Are you sure it's not just gas?" she asked, unable to keep a straight face.

"I'm sure," I said. "And I'm trying to spill my guts here so if you don't mind holding the jokes-"

"Sorry." She raised a hand to my cheek. "I'm not trying to make light of what you're saying. I know it's sincere. And I feel it, too. I just don't want us to feel any more pressure. We have time now, and we're together. So let's just enjoy it and not try to speed up the clock."

"Is that a yes?"

She smiled. "Of course it's a yes."

My chest loosened. "Perfect."

"There's just one little problem," she said, rocking up on her tippy toes.

I furrowed my brow. "What's that?"

"I don't know if I'd be comfortable living in a place where I hadn't been fucked on the kitchen counter."

"Totally understandable," I said, lifting her waist and setting her ass down next to the sink.

"Oh good," she said, hanging her arms around my neck. "I was worried you might think I was being a diva."

I shook my head. "Not at all. And I agree this is a situation we should correct immediately."

She leaned forward to whisper in my ear as her hands found my belt. "Then correct it already, Ethan. I've been wet for you all night."

FORTY NINE
- Jenny -

I was down on my knees framing one of the New York skyline prints when Ethan came up with more frames from the car.

"Oh good," I said. "I was hoping you got some red ones. I think they'll look great with those."

He furrowed his brow. "The ones of you?"

"Yeah." I leaned the picture I'd just framed against the coffee table and sat back on my heels. "You don't agree?"

"Those aren't for sale."

I pressed my palms on my thighs. "What do you mean those aren't for sale?"

"I mean the print I did of you sitting naked for me isn't for anyone's eyes but mine."

"Don't be silly," I said, getting to my feet. "You can't even tell it's me, and it's such a good one."

He started sorting the frames on the kitchen counter. "Absolutely not."

I wiped my forehead on the back of my hand. "Look, Ethan, I'm flattered at your possessiveness, but you have to put at least one of those in."

"No I don't."

"But I'll sit for you anytime! And you still have the lino stamp. You can make more if you want whenever."

"I told you," he said. "They're a limited edition."

I folded my arms.

He glanced up at me. "I'm not changing my mind on this."

"You are," I said, walking over and laying my hand over his so he'd stop sorting frames. "This is your shot. Your moment. You have to stand out from the other people showcasing their work, and that print sexes up the whole collection."

"My skylines are sexy enough."

I craned my head forward. "Look at me."

He clenched his jaw and fixed his eyes on mine.

"Trust me on this. Please."

"I don't see why I should put it up if I wouldn't sell it."

"Because you will sell it," I said. "For a pretty penny, too."

He shook his head.

"Oh c'mon. Everything has a price," I said. "Except for the memory we have of making it, and you can't showcase that anyway."

"Too bad. That would really turn out a crowd."

I sighed. "You know I'm right."

"It's personal."

"No it's not." I ran my hand through my hair. "That's what you don't understand because you haven't shown your work to enough people yet. Once you see that it's personal to them, you'll understand why you don't lose anything by sharing it."

He raised his eyebrows. "Are you done?"

I pointed at the red and yellow print of my back. "Someone is going to look at that, and they're not going to see me. They're going to see someone they love. And that little boy with the boat is going to mean something entirely different to someone else than whatever it means to you."

"Not much."

I rolled my eyes. "You get my point, though."

"I do."

"How about you do it my way this once- just to humor me- and I'll shut up about it after the exhibition."

He dropped his chin. "You'll shut up about it?"

I nodded.

"Well I'd be a fool not to take you up on that offer."

"Great. It's settled." I reached for one of the red frames and tiptoed through the minefield of stacked prints to get back to the ones of me.

A second later, there was a knock on the door.

I looked at him with wide eyes.

His expression was the same.

I shrugged and shook my head. Lord knows I wasn't expecting anyone. No one even knew I was here.

Ethan moved for the peephole, and when he turned back to me, his eyes were squeezed shut.

"Who is it?" I whispered.

He looked pissed for a second, but he hid his sulky expression before he opened the door.

"Hi Vicky," he said.

My back went straight. "Mom?"

She looked at me over Ethan's shoulder as she gave him a hug, her eyes sweeping across the room.

My stomach sank at how gutted Ethan must've felt that his prints were everywhere.

"What's all this?" she asked, opening her arms towards me.

I hopped back across the room and gave her a hug.

It felt nice to have her arms around me. She was a good hugger- even though she still hugged me like I was five. I looked over her shoulder at Ethan and mouthed the word sorry.

"It's for an art show," Ethan said.

"I see." She turned around and bent every which way, straining to admire the framed and unframed prints. "It's a wonderful collection."

I elbowed him behind her back.

"I love that one over there," she said, pointing to the print we'd just been arguing about.

"Ethan made them," I blurted.

She turned around with a hand over her chest. "What?"

"He's an artist. Surprise."

She shook her head. "Ethan, honey, these are remarkable. I had no idea you were still interested in art."

He shrugged.

"Speaking of surprises," I said. "What are you doing here, Mom?"

She pulled her sunglasses off her head and started folding them. "Ed wanted to go to a WW2 Auction in Pittsburgh with Uncle Jim."

I cocked my head. "Uh-huh."

"And I didn't want him driving all that way on his own." She tucked her glasses in the top of her shirt.

I furrowed my brow. "So you made him drive even further?"

She waved her hands at me. "It's only another five hours, and I haven't seen you in months."

I pursed my lips.

"Plus, I need a new pair of boots."

I squinted at her.

"But mostly I just wanted to see you guys!" She smiled. "You both look wonderful by the way."

"Where's my dad?" Ethan asked.

"He went to pick up some lunch." She glanced at her watch. "He didn't want to show up empty handed after he sent Jenny here under false pretenses."

Ethan scoffed.

"Speaking of false pretenses, Mom-"

She raised her eyebrows.

I swallowed the lump in my throat. "Ethan and I have something to tell you."

Ethan laid his hand on my shoulder. "Jenny."

I looked at him. "We have to tell her. Besides, she'll know the best way to break the news to your dad."

He sighed.

"What's going on?" my mom asked, shifting her weight.

I took a deep breath. "Ethan and I are dating."

Her eyes grew wide. "Dating who?"

"Each other," I said, standing as tall as I could.

She looked back and forth between us. "How long has this been going on?"

Ethan stepped up and rested his hand on my lower back.

I felt like I wasn't even in my own body, like I'd be able to plead insanity if she freaked out. "Since shortly after I arrived."

She leaned a hip against the counter and crossed her arms.

I thought I would faint before she broke the silence.

"I thought this might happen," she said softly.

I raised my eyebrows. "What?"

She shrugged. "I can't speak for Ethan, of course, but I suppose you've been hiding your feelings for long enough so-"

"What?! You knew?!" I shook my head. "But-"

She scrunched her face. "I may have read your diary once or twice."

My mouth fell open. "Once or twice?! What the hell, Mom?!"

"How else was I supposed to make sure you weren't using drugs?"

I furrowed my brow. "I don't know! Freaking ask me maybe?!"

"Relax, Jenny. It's not like I made photocopies."

My hands went to my head. "Photocopies?! You shouldn't have read it."

"True," she said. "But you also shouldn't have left it around like any old book."

"That's no excuse! God. Has everyone had a skim through my diary?" I spun around and looked at Ethan.

"What about you? Did it ever fall open in front of you?"

He looked down between his feet.

I smacked him in the chest.

"Once," he said, turning red. "Better than once or twice, though, right?" he asked, glancing at my mom.

I slapped my fists down at my sides. "Unbelievable."

"Calm down," my mom said. "It wasn't exactly a page turner."

I covered my face with my hands.

"Sorry," she said. "I shouldn't have mentioned it."

"No," I huffed. "You shouldn't have."

She raised her palms like white flags. "What I meant to say was, congratulations. You two have my full support."

I rolled my eyes.

"Thanks, Vicky," Ethan said, putting a hand on my waist and squeezing me against him. "Let's hope my dad is as understanding as you've been."

FIFTY
- Ethan -

My dad was people watching like an obvious tourist when I joined him in the beer garden.

"What the hell is that?" he asked when I set his pint down.

"It's a pint," I said, sliding it to him across the picnic table.

"It's a pitcher."

"This is New York."

"I realize that," he said. "But a pint is standard measure of-"

"I know what a pint is. But this is New York. You don't have to drink all of it if you don't want."

He sighed. "I just don't want to overdo it. I told the girls I'd take them to a show tonight if they didn't get heat exhaustion while they were out shopping."

"Well, depending on the show, you might decide to skull the whole thing."

"Mmm." He lifted it and took a sip.

"You don't know what you're seeing yet?"

He shook his head. "I left it up to the girls." He furrowed his brow. "Do you want to come?"

"Depends on the show, I guess." I scooted towards the brick wall beside the table and leaned my back against it. My dad looked older than I remembered, like time was accelerating when we were apart. I wondered if he felt the same about me.

"So… that's a lot of art in your apartment."

I pursed my lips and nodded. "A few year's worth."

"You never really stopped?"

I shook my head.

"Why did you keep it a secret?"

I turned an ear towards him. "You're joking, right?"

"Joking?"

"Oh right. You don't do jokes."

"Enlighten me."

I sighed. "After Mom died, there was no one around who wanted to see my stuff anymore. And you grew to detest it. Like it reminded you of her or something."

He took a sip of his beer and smacked his lips. "I'm sorry, Ethan."

I flipped my sunglasses down over my eyes.

"I know it's too little too late, but I didn't exactly put your grieving before my own."

I shrugged. "You did your best."

"I shouldn't have sent you away, though," he said. "I should've stuck up for you at the school and-"

"That wasn't your fault. Really. And it was the right call."

His lips formed a straight line.

"I'm not going to thank you for it or anything because it sucked, but I was never going to get out of that town the way I was going."

"Well, it does seem like you've made something of yourself."

"I'm a work in progress."

"For what it's worth, I'm glad you kept up with the art… even though I'm too thick to get it."

"Apology accepted." I took a sip of my beer.

He did the same.

I wished it could be more natural with him and me.

Ben had drinks with his dad several times a month. They played tennis together and everything. But my dad and I were so forced, as if we were always trying not to reveal too much.

I didn't know if it was that my mom was the only thing we ever really had in common or if it was normal for men to have complicated relationships with their fathers. Regardless, there was a reason I didn't take him for a fucking coffee.

"Get anything good at the auction?" I asked.

"I outbid your Uncle Jim for a Zippo that belonged to some general."

"Because you wanted it or because you can't resist a little competition?"

"Both," he said. "But I'll probably give it to him for his birthday."

"That's nice."

"I'm keeping the bosun whistle I got for myself, though. I'm going to get it cleaned up and put it on display in the front room."

"Don't get it too cleaned up. Those things can lose their value if-"

"Thanks, Ethan, but I'm not an idiot," he said. "And you can stop pretending you give a shit about my collection."

"I figured it was the least I could do after you pretended to care about my art stuff."

"I do care about your art stuff," he said. "I just don't know how to show it."

"Don't feel you have to."

"I wish I could," he said. "But caring about our family takes so much of my energy that there's not much left for me to spend getting excited about paint brushes."

"Don't worry about it."

"What else is new?" he asked. "How are things going with work?"

"Good. I like my job. It pays well. I hang out with attractive people all day who treat me like I'm their favorite person."

He nodded. "Whatever floats your boat."

I bit the inside of my cheek.

"What about Jenny?"

I pushed my sunglasses back on my head. "What do you mean?"

"I mean I want to know why all three of you were thick as thieves when I showed up at your apartment."

I swallowed.

"Christ. I'm highly trained in interrogation, Ethan. You think I can't tell when someone's trying to avoid telling me something?"

"Promise you won't freak out."

"I haven't freaked out since '98."

I raised my eyebrows. "More like ninety eight seconds ago."

"Whatever. I won't raise my voice anyway. It's bad for my blood pressure."

"Jenny and I are dating."

"Dating who?"

"Each other."

He raised his aviators and squinted at me. "What do you mean you're dating?"

"I mean we're living together as boyfriend and girlfriend."

He turned his ear towards me. "Does she sleep in your bed?"

I let my head fall back against the bricks.

"Wow. That is news," he said, wrapping his shovel hands around his glass. "No wonder you guys were all atwitter."

"Whatever that means," I mumbled.

"And things are going well?"

"I've never been happier."

He nodded and took a sip of his beer. "How'd Vicky take it?"

"Surprisingly well."

"Mmm. She warned me this might happen."

"What?"

"Not in so many words, but Jesus. Women's intuition, eh? It's arguably more powerful than my best interrogation tactics."

I squinted at him. "What do you mean she warned you?"

"That was a poor choice of words. It would be more accurate to say she suspected there was something going between you two."

I craned my neck forward. "Go on."

"After you shipped off, Jenny was depressed for weeks."

"Depressed?"

"Just not herself, you know. No singing in the shower. No back talk. That kind of thing."

"Yeah."

"Very strange for a girl that age."

"Uh-huh."

"I thought she might be on drugs or something. Downers. Maybe a bit of skunk here and there. Wouldn't have surprised me for all that time she spent with what's her face with the raccoon eyes."

"Brandi."

"Yeah."

"Anyway, Vicky said Jenny wasn't on drugs. She was just heartbroken."

I furrowed my brow. "Seriously?"

"I chocked it up to hormones and didn't try to understand. You were only kids."

I took a sip of beer.

"Was it the same for you?" he asked. "Even then?"

I nodded. "Yeah. It was. And when you guys got married everything got so confused."

"Understandable."

I scratched the back of my head.

He sighed. "I'm not one of those guys that takes young love seriously, but there must be something there if it hasn't gone away after all this time."

"We think so."

He furrowed his brow. "You love her?"

I nodded.

"Does she know?"

"More or less."

He raised a finger at me. "Make sure she knows," he said. "I swear to god the only peace I had after your mother died was that I told her I loved her that morning."

A lump formed in my throat.

"So don't miss an opportunity to show her how much you care. Never put it off. Never skip a day. Take it from me, life is too short to assume the people you love know it."

I swallowed.

"And I'm sorry if you felt you had to put your love on hold because of decisions I made- not that I wouldn't make the same decisions again because I love Vicky very much-"

"I know."

"Anyway, it's not for me to judge what's best when it comes to matters of the heart. I've made a lot of mistakes in my life, but if there's anything I've learned, it's that you don't apologize for love and you don't hide it away."

"Thanks, Dad."

"And I'll stop myself there before you lose all respect for me."

I smiled.

Then he stood up and pointed at my glass. "Same again?"

Epilogue
Jenny

Three months later...

Ethan had pulled his jeep into the alley behind the studio and was stacking the unsold prints in the back.

"I'd say that was a massive success," I said, cocking a hip. "Wouldn't you?"

"I had my doubts going in," he said, closing the trunk.

"Oh?"

"I didn't expect people to come knowing it would only be my stuff."

I raised my eyebrows. "Well come they did. They ran out of canapes and everything!"

He smiled and walked around to the passenger side to open my door. "I suspect that's because you spent more time circling the canapes than you did selling my work."

I stopped beside the open door. "First of all, your prints sell themselves. Second of all, you should be grateful anyone noticed anything with those bacon wrapped whatsits in the room."

He rolled his eyes. "Get in, will ya?"

I climbed in and moved my legs so he could close the door. I couldn't believe he was still doing things like holding doors open for me, but I wasn't complaining.

Besides, it's not like I asked him to make such a fuss. He just did it. Like it wasn't even a chore, though I almost wished he'd just get in the car at the exact same time that I did so I wouldn't have to miss a moment talking to him.

"I can't believe that daisies print sold for six hundred bucks!" I said when he slid in the driver's seat.

"You and me both." He turned the key in the ignition and checked his mirrors. "It's like I have some sort of lucky charm." He smiled and looked at me out of the corner of his eye.

"Do you think Ben meant what he said about hanging some of the skyline prints at the club?"

"I do," he said, rolling down the alley towards the main street. "And I think if Carrie okays the idea, he'll follow through with it."

"I'm sure she will," I said. "In fact, I bet if I gave Nora one for Carrie's office, she'd be putting them in her client's homes in no time."

"That's a great idea."

"Right?!"

"I was thinking," he said, waiting for a gap in traffic to open up. "That following the success of my recent shows, it's probably about time we celebrated my listening to you in the first place."

"What do you mean?" I asked, turning towards him.

"I mean none of this would've happened if you hadn't forced me at gunpoint to let other people see my stuff."

I rolled my eyes.

"And you put in a lot of work to get me those first few opportunities."

"Mostly the first one, but-"

"Still," he said. "All your encouragement has gone to my head."

"Good. It's about damn time."

He pulled up at the light and rubbed his fingers along the blue paint spot on his steering wheel. "In fact, I felt so good going into tonight that I bought you a little something yesterday."

I raised my eyebrows. "Can I eat it?"

"No."

"Can I wear it?"

"No."

I furrowed my brow. "Are you sure it's for me?"

"Technically it's for us both."

"What is it?"

He leaned his head back. "Check the pocket behind my seat."

I reached behind him and slipped my hand in the tight leather pocket.

"Got it yet?" he asked.

"It better not be a dirty tissue that I left in here or something because I already apologized for forgetting the fast food trash last-"

He laughed. "It's not a dirty tissue, Jenny. Christ. But if that's where you've set your expectations, I feel confident that you're going to be pleased."

I stretched my fingers and squeezed my eyes shut. "Oh wait- I feel something." I slid the thick paper until I could get a grip on it and pulled it into the front seat.

He glanced at me.

"What is it?" I asked, staring at the pamphlet.

The picture on the front was of two people drinking cocktails on a beach surrounded by nothing but pristine blue water and swaying palm trees.

Well, they weren't really swaying, but it seemed like they would've been based on how the woman's dress was blowing in the breeze. Then again, I'd never seen a real palm tree in my life. Maybe they were too heavy to sway.

"Open it."

I flipped the pamphlet open and let my eyes travel along the tropical font. "The Abbott Hotel Bermuda."

"Looks nice, right?"

"Yeaaah."

"Glad you think so."

I turned an ear towards him. "Are we going there?"

"We are, actually."

I raised my eyebrows. "Wait seriously? To this place? In Bermuda?!"

"It's going to get cold soon, and I'm dreading the thought of you wearing more clothes."

I smiled. "So you're taking me to Bermuda?!"

"That's right. For two weeks at the beginning of next month. I already got you a window seat."

"You what?!"

He cocked his head. "Don't tell me you prefer the aisle?"

"What? No! I don't know! I can't even remember the last time I was on a plane."

He pulled along the curb behind a taxi. "But you'll go with me, right? Cause two for one drinks only make sense when you're with-"

I scrunched my face.

"What?"

"I can't."

"What do you mean you can't?"

"I got a job."

He craned his neck forward. "What?"

"You know that audition I went to for the Lion King two weeks ago?"

"Yeah."

"They're going to let me be a hyena."

His hands went to his head. "Oh my god, Jenny, that's fantastic! Why didn't you tell me?!"

"I only found out this morning, and I thought it would make more sense to tell you after your show so-"

He lunged across the center console and threw his arms around me. "Congratulations. I'm so proud of you. Oh my god." He leaned back in his seat. "I can't believe you're going to be a hyena. I can't wait to tell everyone!"

"Hyena number two to be exact."

He was smiling so hard I thought his face might tear in half. "Holy Shit. That's the best hyena!"

I rolled my eyes.

"It's about damn time your talent got recognized. Are you so pumped or what? "

I shrugged. "I don't think it's quite sunk in yet."

"You're going to be great."

"I figure worst case scenario, I mess up my lines and just laugh really hard and no one will know-"

"You're a genius!"

"And you are ridiculously supportive."

"I knew you were a fucking star." He shook his head out the windshield. "Hyena number two. I'll be damned."

"Anyway, the rehearsals start in two weeks so I can't go to Bermuda."

"Don't worry about it. We'll go another time."

I raised my eyebrows. "Yeah?"

"Of course. We can't fuck off in the middle of your big break. Besides, the oceans aren't rising that fast. Bermuda will still be there after the final curtain."

"Cause it's not that I don't want to go."

He put a hand on my shoulder. "You don't have to explain, Jenny. Or would you rather I start calling you Hyena number two to help you get in character?"

"Shut up."

"We have to celebrate."

"Agreed, but nothing seems exciting after your Bermuda surprise."

He pursed his lips and turned the flashing blinkers on to buy us more curb time. "We could always go for drinks?"

"And not stop until we're so drunk we feel like we're on an island in the Caribbean?"

"It's an idea," he said.

"I was craving bottomless margaritas earlier this week."

"I can do one better."

I raised my eyebrows. "I'm listening."

"How about we go back to the apartment and drink margaritas bottomless," he said. "That's all I wanted to do in Bermuda anyway."

I smiled. "I love that idea."

"I was hoping you might."

"And I love you, too."

He smiled. "Admitting it is the first step to recovery."

I shook my head. "I don't want to recover. I've never felt better."

He flashed his eyebrows and pulled back into traffic. "Just wait till we get home."

"I can't wait," I said. "I'm too excited."

"I know the feeling," he said, keeping his eyes on the road.

And as I stared at the man behind the wheel, I was overwhelmed with an optimism that filled me so full of happiness there was no room for anything else.

Because of him.

Because being his girl was my role of a lifetime.

Other books in the Soulmates Series

My Best Friend's Brother
A Friends To Lovers Romance

The Boy Next Door
A Small Town Romance

First Love
A Second Chance Romance

Printed in Great
Britain
by Amazon